THE BUSY BODY

Anne really knew little about Peter, the man she had just married after a short courtship. A man who looks just like Peter appears — could he be a twin? An ex-girlfriend makes Anne nervous and insecure.

Burglaries are occurring which seem planned, as valuable jewellery is stolen. Is Peter involved in this? Who is telling the truth?

THE BUSY BODY

Elizabeth Ferrars

First published 1962
by
William Collins

This edition 2001 by Chivers Press
published by arrangement with
the author's estate

ISBN 0 7540 8583 X

British Library Cataloguing in Publication Data available

Printed and bound in Great Britain by
Redwood Books, Trowbridge, Wiltshire

CHAPTER I

AT LAST the big Jaguar, which had hung on the tail of our Austin Seven for a surprisingly long time, sailed past us. Immediately afterwards Peter stopped at a pub with pumps and said that we needed petrol. It didn't look to me as if we did, since we had only a few miles more to go. But as he got out of the car, he added that we might as well have a drink too while we were about it, so I thought that it really must be for the drink that we had stopped and that for some reason he was nervous.

He might, I thought, have said so in the first place. But I was learning that there were things about which Peter couldn't help being devious, although the suggestion that we should stop for a drink wouldn't normally have been one of them. He wasn't ordinarily a nervous person. There was generally the serenity of a confident child on his clever, eager face. Yet at the moment it was clear that he had something on his mind about the visit ahead of us which was causing him discomfort and the drink was either to drown this or to help him confide in me.

He wasn't, at that stage of our lives, very good at confiding in me. But we had been married for only a week and had known each other only for four, so if our understanding of one another had a certain unevenness, if there were thin patches in it and here and there great holes, it was really only natural and nothing much to worry about. This, at least, was what I sometimes told myself.

Opening the door on my side of the car, I got out into the glare of the sunshine in the pub's nearly empty car-park. Only a small van was there before us and there seemed to be no one about to attend to the pumps.

Leaving Peter to discover the attendant, or else to find out that on a Sunday there wasn't one, I said that I would meet him in the bar and made my way to the ladies' room.

The pub was on the main road to Lachester, just before a roundabout. It was called the White Horse and was a modern place, with neat rose-beds in front of it and a gravel drive. The building was of red brick, with picture-windows, a revolving door and an elaborate portico, supported by brick pillars shaped like cork-screws. Inside, the wallpaper on every single wall was different and it all smelt of one of those powerfully scented floor polishes. It wasn't the kind of pub at which I should have chosen to stop, if Peter had asked me. However, I didn't think that he had chosen it because of any special liking for it, but only because of a sudden urgency to unburden himself to me which, just as we had happened to reach the place, had made it seem imperative to stop.

I knew by then that there was very little foresight in Peter's nature and almost no patience. Outside of his work, that is to say. I suppose a historian must have plenty of both, and he was supposed to be a promising one. But apart from that, when an idea came into his head, he appeared to act upon it immediately, or else simply forget it. I had realised that this wasn't likely to make him easy to live with, but I was trying hard to get used to it, as I was trying to get used to the whole amazing business of being married. And that brings me to a point about myself which I think is important.

It is that as I stood in the pale pink and black cloak-room, with its glittering plumbing; as I combed my hair and put on fresh lipstick, my state of mind wasn't normal. The excitement of these last few weeks had buffeted me into a kind of stupor and the happiness which at times seemed almost too much for me and from which I felt occasional crazy impulses to fly for my life, had produced in me something that resembled a drugged condition, in which nothing was capable of seeming strange.

That was why it didn't seem excessively strange, but only horrible in a matter-of-fact and not at all impossible way, when I went into the bar a few minutes later and saw Peter there, red in the face, glassy-eyed and drunk.

I ought to have known that it wasn't possible. We had separated five minutes before and he had been as sober as I was. So either he wasn't drunk or he wasn't Peter.

Yet all I could do was stand there, stare stupidly and say, " Why, Peter . . . ! "

He looked at me with Peter's dark brown eyes with the dark fringe of lashes and the small lines fanning out from their corners across his temples; lines cut somewhat deeply already for a face otherwise so smooth and young. He gave me Peter's smile. That is to say, it began as Peter's smile, but then it went slipping too far across his narrow face, showing not only his rather irregular, white teeth but a stretch of pink gum and the tip of a tongue that came out and slid uneasily along his lower lip.

He gave his head a confused shake. He frowned. It was Peter's frown that furrowed his high forehead with the fair, slightly curly hair that flopped forward on to it.

But it wasn't Peter's voice which said in a belligerent tone, " Peter Piper! "

This voice was throaty and thick, with a good deal of cockney in it. And I had had time by then to take in the fact that this man wasn't wearing Peter's grey suit, white shirt and blue tie, but a red polo-necked sweater and flannel trousers, both shabby and oil-stained.

" Peter Piper picked a peck of bloody something, didn't he? " the unfamiliar voice demanded, rising as he asked this question, not of me, but of a man, wearing a loose brown overall and old felt hat, who was standing with one elbow on the bar and his hand folded around a double whisky. " Didn't he? . . . I said to you, didn't he, eh? "

" Pepper," the man in the overall said indifferently. " Pickled pepper."

He was short and squat, with grey bristles sprouting on an unshaven chin, a leathery face and little, sharp, furtive eyes. He and a man polishing glasses behind the bar were the only other people there. The time was only just after twelve o'clock and the place had been open for only a few minutes.

" See what I mean? " the strange voice said out of Peter's mouth to the man behind the bar. " If I can say that, I'm all right, see."

" Only you didn't say it—Mr. Biggs said it," said this man, who was tall and very tweedily dressed, with a purplish face and a sagging paunch contained in a yellow pullover. " I'd take care when you get on that bike of yours, young fellow."

His smile was genial but his eyes were watchful and worried. He was worried not only by the young man getting drunk in his shiny red-and-chromium bar, but by me and the way that I was standing there, staring.

I was angry, so furiously angry that in my head I had already been making plans for leaving Peter. Nothing on earth was going to induce me to stay married to a man who was liable to play this ghastly sort of practical joke. For that was how I was thinking then of what was happening. It seemed a little more possible that Peter was a quick-change artist with a dreadful sense of humour than that someone else should share his dark brown eyes and nearly golden hair, his aquiline nose and irregular teeth and be his height and have his slender, vigorous body.

But to say that what I was doing as I looked at him was thinking is an exaggeration. I simply saw him and hated him for a disappointment too intense to be faced yet. I hurt all over with the force of this hatred. But as soon as I had control of my petrified muscles again, I was going to walk straight out of his life.

Most of this the landlord must have seen. He must have been sure a scene was coming.

" Now look," he said peaceably to the young man, " you don't really want a drink, do you? Why don't you go out and take a turn in the garden? Lovely day. Take a look at my roses. I've some nice roses."

Throatily, the young man told him what he could do with his roses.

The man in the brown overall, whom the landlord had called Mr. Biggs, looked at me with a quivering little grin lifting one corner of his mouth. If a scene was coming, he was going to enjoy it.

" I want a drink, Mr. Galpin," he said. " It's thirsty weather and it isn't your job to quarrel with a man's thirst, is it? " He emptied his glass at a gulp and pushed it across the counter.

The young man was looking at me again, frowning and trying to concentrate.

" She comes in here and she calls me Peter and tells me I'm pickled," he said carefully, as if he were taking great pains to be fair to me. " It's sort of clever, when you come to think of it. Takes you by surprise. Well then, come and have a drink with Peter—come on, come on! " He leant towards me and caught one of my hands.

Two things happened then. One was that I suddenly knew for certain that the hard hand, grasping mine and pulling me forward, was not a hand that had ever touched me before. The second thing was the appearance from behind me of a red-haired girl in a white cotton water-proof, who struck the wrist of the young man a sharp, chopping blow with the side of her hand and asked him acridly what the hell he thought he was getting up to now.

He answered sulkily that he wasn't getting up to anything, but all at once he seemed in a hurry to be gone. Picking up a wind-jacket and cycling helmet from a chair, he gripped the girl by the shoulder and pushed her towards the door. He was steadier on his feet than I should have expected from his speech, but all the same I didn't envy the girl if she was going to ride on his pillion.

It might have been some thought of this that made her pause in the doorway, resisting his thrusting hand, and look back at us uncertainly.

She was only about nineteen. She was small, with a small, fierce face, as white and corpse-like as heavy make-up could make it, and greenish eyes that looked at us out of black frames of mascara. Her red hair was fluffed out round her head into a shape something like a tea-cosy. Her coat was so short that she seemed to be all long, pale legs, ending in shoes with incredible points and heels like daggers. She had the rough vitality of a terrier puppy. Yet suddenly there was a look of helplessness about her, of shrinking.

" Come on, come on! " the young man said, giving her another push and she turned and went out with him. From outside the door, I caught the sound of their voices, raised in shrill quarrelling.

I heard the landlord mutter, " Thank the lord for that. Came in here drunk already and with that kid in tow. I don't care for that sort of thing."

" Well, Mr. Galpin, you're a rum fellow," said the man in the brown overall. " Only man I know who quarrels with his own livelihood. If he doesn't get the stuff here, he'll get it elsewhere."

" I can do without customers like him," the landlord answered. " I do well enough out of you, George. Ready for another? "

The other man pushed his glass back again.

Filling it, Mr. Galpin noticed me and seemed to wonder why I hadn't gone out after the others. He didn't look too pleased that I hadn't.

" Yes? Anything I can do for you? " he asked.

It was at that moment that Peter, the real Peter, came into the room.

He came in with his usual look of cheerful detachment from his surroundings. He was clear-eyed and quite sober. It wasn't in him to notice that he had walked into any unusual situation and that he was being stared at by the other two men with looks almost superstitious in their astonishment.

" There's a nice garden out there," he said. " Let's get our drinks and take them out in the sun. I want to talk to you."

I was feeling a kind of astonishment too that I could ever have mistaken the man in the red pullover for him, for I was so dazzled by relief at seeing him again as he really was that the other image almost immediately faded. There was something dreamlike already about the whole experience. After a moment I could hardly believe that it had happened at all and that for a few horrible minutes I had utterly lost Peter. I began to feel abjectly guilty for my faithlessness and wasn't sure if I wanted to laugh or cry.

" Whew! " Mr. Biggs said, putting his glass down abruptly. " I wouldn't have believed it. If it wasn't that this is only my second . . ."

" Third, George."

Mr. Galpin was still staring, but he took Peter's appearance more calmly than the other. He would probably take most things calmly. But the eyes in his purplish, pouchy face glistened with interest.

" Now we know why the young lady stood there, looking as if she'd seen a ghost," Mr. Biggs said. " And for all you know, perhaps that's just exactly what she did.

I wouldn't be surprised. I can tell you . . ." His leathery face became very earnest and he sidled a little way along the bar towards Peter, trying to look him in the eyes and hold his gaze. " I can tell you of experiences I've had myself, sir, when I was in the East, which wouldn't make you scoff at that explanation. Meeting a man and talking to him once when I was on leave in Bombay and then hearing—and no doubt about it, mind, everything on the up and up and absolutely vouched for by a man I happened to know who was a judge and an educated man of the highest reputation—well, he swore this fellow I'm telling you about had been back in England at the time. Actually under arrest for a very nasty robbery with violence. So what do you make of that? I'll tell you what *I* make of it? I think it was this man's other self I saw. We've all got other selves. There's a name for them, only at the moment I don't just happen to recall it. And with some people, this other self is, as you might say, not properly under control and when there's trouble about, it's liable to be seen in some queer places."

Peter listened to this with attention. He didn't seem surprised by it. He was very seldom surprised by anything that anyone could say or do. Almost the only thing that roused real astonishment in him was the way that inanimate objects wouldn't remain where he was sure that he had left them.

" That could have been awfully useful to your friend as an alibi, if he'd known about it," he said.

" No, no, sir, I'm serious," Mr. Biggs said, with a look of offence. " I could tell you other things that have happened to me——"

" Now, George," the landlord interrupted. " I'm sorry, sir, if we stared at you a bit hard, but as the young lady can tell you, it was quite startling when you walked in just now. Did you know you've got a double? "

Peter looked at me questioningly and I said, " Yes,

there was a man in here just now who could easily have
been your twin."

" Didn't you meet him as you came in? " the landlord
asked.

" I saw someone getting on to a motor-bike, but he'd
a helmet on," Peter said. " Can we have some sandwiches
in the garden? " He appeared far less interested in his
double than I should have expected. Yet he seemed in
a hurry to get outside and that wasn't like him. He liked
gossiping with strangers. A long-standing appointment
never seemed quite as important to him as the chance
meeting that turned out entertaining.

But I had another problem to think of just then, which
was why we had really stopped at the White Horse, so
as we went out and crossed a terrace towards a bench in
the sunny angle of the wall, I said, " I thought we were
going to have lunch with your mother, Peter."

He answered absently, " Oh, she won't worry if we
turn up a bit later."

" She's used to it, is she, poor woman? " I said. " I hope
you don't think I'll ever get used to it."

" What?—Oh well, I suppose she is used to it." He
smiled. " I mean she really is, you know. She doesn't
mind."

" When I'm expecting someone——"

" But she won't be expecting us," he said quickly.
" She'll just wait till we turn up, then if we haven't
eaten she'll throw something together—or Mrs. Joy will.
It's quite all right. And I want to talk to you before
we get there." We sat down side by side on the bench.
The sun had made it warm to the touch and there was
a humming of insects in the air. " First, though, tell
me what happened in there, Anne? "

" I saw someone I thought was you," I said. " I actually
spoke to him and called him Peter."

" You mean he was really as like me as that? "

"He really was." I tried to laugh, but the sound wasn't very convincing. "Who is he, Peter? Have you a twin brother?"

"It sounds rather as if perhaps I have," Peter said.

"Now look," I said, "I agree you're entitled to a certain amount of scholarly absent-mindedness in your profession, but surely you can remember a thing like that."

"It isn't a case of remembering," he said, "it's quite simply not being absolutely sure—because of having been adopted. I did have a twin brother, as a matter of fact." He picked up one of my hands. From the way he gently touched one finger after the other, he might have been counting them to make sure that I had the right number. "But as I've told you, I know hardly anything about my real family. I don't know if he's alive or dead. So it isn't impossible, I suppose, that you saw him. I mean, if we're really so alike that you mistook him for me. Now tell me, what was the matter with him?"

"The matter . . . ?"

"You didn't like him."

I felt the surprise I usually felt when I encountered Peter's perceptiveness. I wasn't accustomed to living with someone who occasionally had so much, and yet at times went into states of such total unawareness of what anyone around him was thinking or feeling that it became easy to assume that he never noticed such things.

"I think it was mainly the shock of the thing," I said, "my being *able* to mistake you. It's an eerie sort of feeling."

"Afraid it could happen again?"

I laughed and was starting to say that I didn't really think it could, when we saw Mr. Galpin coming towards us along the terrace with our drinks and a plate of sandwiches.

Standing looking down at us as Peter fished in his

pockets for money, Mr. Galpin gave a wheezy chuckle.

" Believe it or not, sir, this is the first time in my life I've felt inclined to doubt the evidence of my senses," he said. " Without going all the way with George Biggs about other selves and what-not, I did for a minute feel I was seeing double. Not a nice feeling for a man in my trade, eh? "

" I'm sorry I missed it all," Peter said, with the same unconcern as he had shown in the bar. " Do you happen to know who he was? "

" Can't say I remember seeing him before," the big man answered, " though there's something familiar about his face. But perhaps that's because you've been in sometime? "

" I don't think I have," Peter said.

" I thought I didn't recognise you. But I haven't been at this job long—used to be in the Air Force till my heart started playing tricks—and I'm not as good at faces as I ought to be. I'll remember you next time, anyway! "

Chuckling again, he went off to attend to some other people who had strolled out on to the terrace and were admiring his roses.

I bit into a chicken sandwich. " You're being awfully cagey about it all, Peter," I said. " Are you really not very interested? "

" Only afraid of becoming much too interested," he answered slowly. " Afraid of doing something rather absurd about it."

I realised then that I had been stupid in not recognising how much he was afraid of yielding at once to an immense temptation.

" And I've always thought your having been adopted wasn't very important to you," I said. " Except that . . . yes, come to think of it, you mentioned it the very first time we met."

" Oh yes, actually it's always seemed to me a very

important thing about myself—when I've happened to think of it at all. And I thought of it then because I knew you were going to be very important too."

" But you don't mind about it, do you? " I asked.

I had never seen any sign that he minded, and I knew that he had a strong affection for his adopted mother, whom we were on our way to visit.

" Yes, in a rather absurd way I do," he said. " I don't know why. But I've never been able to speak about it naturally, as if I honestly thought it didn't matter. Yet I don't think I could possibly be any fonder of my mother than I am. And my father—well, as he died when I was about five, I don't remember much about him, but what I do remember is all extraordinarily happy."

" So what you mind is the thought of your real family," I said.

" I don't think so." He took a long drink of beer. He had told me once that all he knew about his real family was that he had been born in Portsmouth and that his mother's name had been Ada Hearn. His father's name had not been mentioned on his birth-certificate.

" But this twin brother," I said.

" Well, it's a very odd thing," he said, " I've always had a secret sort of conviction that I'd got a brother somewhere. And I read somewhere or other that that isn't uncommon in twins who've been separated at birth. And after what happened to-day . . ."

He turned his head to take a long look at the pub.

Through its picture-windows we could see that it had been filling up. The bar where I had met the man whom I had mistaken for Peter was crowded with people.

" You know, I think I'll have to try to find him," Peter said. " I hope you aren't going to mind, Anne, even if you didn't like him."

I didn't think it would be any good to say that I minded.

We finished our drinks and our sandwiches and went
back to the car. It was only as we drove off that I
realised that Peter still hadn't told me what he had
wanted to talk about when he stopped at the White
Horse.

CHAPTER II

OUR CAR was a new one, so new, in fact, that this was the
first time that we had driven it out of London. It filled
Peter with pride and joy, because it was the first car that
he had possessed that wasn't more or less tied together
with string. He had ordered it to celebrate fixing up his
first job, after two years on a research grant. The job
was that of assistant lecturer in the modern history department of one of the London colleges and the car had been
waiting for him when he had returned from a rock-
climbing holiday in Austria, the holiday during which
he and I had met.

As we drove out of the car-park, I saw the small van
which had been there when we arrived and I noticed
the name of Geo. Biggs on the side of it. It appeared that
Geo. Biggs was something called a " General Dealer "
in Sandy Green, Lachester, and would give good prices
for almost anything.

Sandy Green turned out to be the suburb of Lachester
which began just beyond the roundabout ahead of us.
I saw the name up over a new post office in a newly made
road of new houses with new, neat little gardens. Beyond
this suburb there was the remnant of an old village
which had been engulfed by the spreading town, then
came playing fields, council houses, a grubby river with
one or two factories beside it, shops, a cinema or two and
in the heart of the town a street of gabled and half-

timbered houses, very handsome except for their shop-fronts, which were those of all the usual chain-stores.

Peter's adopted mother was a doctor, as her dead husband had been also, and her practice was in the town. But her home was on the far side of it, a pleasant-looking white house in an untidy garden, standing almost by itself in a stretch of country obviously soon to be engulfed, but into which at present only one or two new roads had begun to penetrate. When we arrived Dr. Lindsay was sitting in a deck-chair under a tree in the garden. She had a tray, with the remains of some lunch on it, on the grass beside her, a pair of spectacles sitting crookedly on her nose, her eyes shut and her hands folded on top of a book which was lying face downwards on her lap.

Peter tooted his horn gently to waken her. She opened her eyes tranquilly, gave us a little wave, put her book and spectacles down on the ground, heaved herself out of the chair and came to meet us.

At the same time a white poodle appeared out of some bushes behind her and came bounding forward.

It bounded for about ten yards, then came to a dead stop. Looking at me, it quivered all over. Its tail dropped. Its head sank down between its paws. In a crouch of miserable timidity, it slunk away behind the chair that Dr. Lindsay had just left and hid behind it.

She looked back at it. " Silly girl, it's only Peter," she said. " It's Peter—*Peter*, silly! "

The white tail gave one or two nervous thumps on the grass.

Dr. Lindsay turned to me with a smile.

" It's no good, she'll go on hiding till she gets used to you. You'd think, wouldn't you, that she'd been beaten and cowed all her life, but actually we've had her since she was a week-old puppy and I doubt if she's ever even been slapped. It's just her nature—her mysterious female nature. Well, never mind. I'm very glad to see you, Anne. Very glad indeed."

She gave me a firm handshake. She was a short, square, sturdy woman of about sixty, with soft, curly, white hair, grey eyes, plump cheeks and a double chin which hid, at first sight, the line of a powerful jaw. She wore a striped cotton dress which had seen years of service.

Peter kissed her, then went to talk to the poodle, which leapt up at him with squeals of joy, licking his face, but keeping an uneasy eye on me, in case I should advance in her direction.

" Have you had lunch? " Dr. Lindsay asked me, and when I said that we had, she went on, " I didn't wait for you. I make a rule of never waiting for Peter. But I'll get Mrs. Joy to make us some coffee now. I expect you'd like that after your drive."

She had a deep voice, brusque yet friendly. I liked her at sight. I liked her casualness and the way she didn't fuss over me, just because I happened to have become her new daughter-in-law.

Taking me into the house with her, she introduced me to Mrs. Joy, a thin, brisk little woman who came in daily to clean the house and cook Dr. Lindsay's mid-day meal for her. Mrs. Joy had been just about to go home, but she stayed on to make the coffee and I had a far more emotional welcome from her than from Dr. Lindsay, learning that I was a very lucky girl to have got Mr. Peter, because he had far more respect for women than some she could name and if only he wouldn't always leave his shoes in the middle of the floor of whatever room he thought of taking them off in, would be as near perfect as made no matter.

After that Dr. Lindsay and I went out to the garden again, where we found Peter sitting in the deck-chair under the tree with the poodle's head on his knees.

When we appeared, he went to fetch more chairs and cushions, and the poodle darted away into the bushes. " That idiot dog," Dr. Lindsay said as she settled herself. " An imbecile, practically. We ought to have got rid of her years ago, but somehow we got rather fond of her. Or anyway, Peter did, and I got into the habit of putting up with her. She'll get used to you by and by, I expect. I have to admit I feel a little like her myself at this moment. I've been feeling very nervous of this meeting and I dare say you have too."

She gave me a direct glance and the odd thing was that I immediately started to feel nervous. For the glance lingered curiously on my face and was more deliberately diagnostic than felt at all comfortable.

She went on, " Now tell me a little about yourself, Anne. Peter wrote me a hazy description of a meeting on a mountainside in Austria, added that words would not describe you and told me to use my imagination to fill in the gaps—knowing perfectly well that I haven't any. I'm a strictly practical woman."

" You might at least give Anne a little time before you start asking her her name, her age and previous illnesses," Peter said.

She took no notice of him. " Tell me, Anne, are you a rock-climber too? " she asked seriously. " I've been hoping marriage might keep Peter down to safer levels."

" No, I'm not a climber and I can promise you that if there's an easy road up one side of a mountain, I'll never think of struggling up the hard way," I said. " But I don't know if Peter will come with me, or if we'll have to go our own ways and meet at the top."

" He's always been a wretch for climbing up things," Dr. Lindsay said. " Trees, drain-pipes, anything he could find. When I think of how I used to try to control myself, in case my shrieking at him made him fall! "

"I doubt if you've ever shrieked in your life," he said.

"You never noticed if I did, that's certain," she said. "Now tell me about your job, Anne. Peter says you're still going on with it."

I told her that for the present I was, though I had come to no decision yet about the future.

The truth was that since meeting Peter I had thought hardly at all about the future, the past, or about anything but Peter. If we had sometimes made plans, it had never been in a way that could mean anything to anyone but ourselves and we hadn't yet dealt with the question of whether or not I was to give notice to the firm of accountants whose secretary I had been for the last three years, although I vaguely knew that if I didn't pull myself together soon, and give some attention to the world around me, it wouldn't be surprising if the firm gave notice to me.

It was pleasant and peaceful in the garden. The air was full of flower-scents and the droning of bees, while on the grass around us the shadows of the August afternoon lay motionless.

Dr. Lindsay went on shooting direct questions at me about my parents and when they had died, and where I had been to school and so on, and I did my best to answer them. Peter at first talked very little, but presently he started to tell her about the profound joys of driving a new car and seemed to be hopeful that he would be allowed to go on talking about this for the rest of the afternoon. The sound of his cheerful, eager voice made Jess the poodle pluck up her courage and creep out of the bushes, and circling me warily, creep up to give me a cautious sniff. Seeming to find this reassuring, she settled down in a patch of sunshine near my feet and went to sleep.

"There, look at that!" Peter said with a pleased smile

at me. " She usually takes several days at least to get used
to a stranger."

" And sometimes never gets used to them at all, for
no reason anyone can see," Dr. Lindsay said. " For
instance, Owen and Margaret. Even after all this time ...
Oh, by the way, they're going to drop in for a drink
about six o'clock."

" Damn! " Peter said as violently as if he had just
walked into something very hard and very solid.

" Oh well, I don't expect they'll stay for long," Dr.
Lindsay said unconcernedly. She turned to me. " Owen
and Margaret Loader are neighbours of ours. Owen's
a farmer and a writer—you may know his name—and
Margaret was trying to be a writer too, a journalist, until
they got married about six months ago, and bought
the farm on the hill there. We've known Margaret a
very long time. As a matter of fact, she and Peter actually
went to the same kindergarten in Lachester——"

" For God's sake, why did you have to invite them just
to-day? " Peter interrupted.

" They invited themselves," Dr. Lindsay said. " Margaret rang up just about lunch-time."

" And couldn't you have put her off? " he asked. " Just
this once. Couldn't you possibly have done that? "

For the first time I noticed the line of Dr. Lindsay's jaw
under the plump covering of her chins.

" Margaret seemed to know you were coming, though
I'd said nothing about it to her myself," she said. " So
I thought it was you who'd suggested it."

" Of course I didn't suggest it," Peter said. " As if I
would! "

Dr. Lindsay gave a sigh. " Well, I'm sorry, my dear,
I didn't realise you'd mind."

" Can't you put them off? " he said.

" How? " she asked.

" Can't you simply say we don't want them to-day?
Some other time, but not to-day."

" Is that what you'd do yourself? "

" No, I'd probably do something subtle like saying
Anne and I were still in quarantine for bubonic plague! "

She gave him a long, questioning glance and her eyes
grew worried. " The trouble is, Margaret's feelings hurt
very easily, but if you really feel so strongly about it . . ."
She levered herself out of her chair. " I'll see what I
can do, short of being downright rude."

She got up and walked away towards the house.

Looking after her squat figure, Peter muttered something stormy, then reaching out for one of my hands, he
started his trick of counting my fingers. He was thinking hard about something, but it certainly wasn't my
hand.

After a moment I said, " I've got exactly five."

" Five——? "

" Fingers."

He suddenly crushed them all together and pressed them
against his mouth.

Jess, who must have had her eye on us all the time,
even if she was pretending to be asleep, leapt up and
started to bark in a fury of jealousy. Letting go of my
hand, Peter caught hold of her behind the ears, pulled
her towards him and gazed into her eyes. Wagging her
tail, she shot a sidelong glance at me, triumphing over
me.

" Anyway, what's the matter with Margaret? " I
asked. " What did she do to you? "

He went on caressing Jess. " I'll tell you sometime."

" Not now? "

" Please, not now."

I waited a little, then I asked, " Peter, why haven't
you told Dr. Lindsay anything about that man in the
pub? "

He let go of Jess and looked up at me. "Do you think I ought to?"

"I don't know. I've only been wondering why you haven't."

"I'll tell her, if you want me to," he said.

"No, it isn't that. Just why haven't you?—that's all I want to know."

"Well then, I suppose it's because I haven't made up my own mind what I want to do about it," he said. "As a matter of fact, I like to be very clear about a thing before I let my mother get her hands on it. Otherwise she knocks me out before I can get started."

"Yes, I can imagine that," I said.

"But I expect I'll tell her presently. Anne, about Margaret . . ."

"I thought you didn't want to talk about her."

"I don't," he said. "But I know I'll have to, sooner or later. She'll see to that. The way she rang Mother up to-day as soon as she'd seen us. She was the woman who was driving the Jaguar that dogged us for such a long way——"

He stopped because Dr. Lindsay was coming back across the lawn towards us.

"I'm sorry, you're out of luck," she said. "I telephoned, but there's no answer, so I couldn't put them off." She sat down again in her deck-chair and settled a cushion comfortably behind her curly head. "As I said, they won't stay long, because they always visit Owen's mother on a Sunday evening."

"All right—let them come!" Peter said, and Dr. Lindsay smiled, pleased that he had accepted the situation.

But he hadn't really accepted it and soon she saw this and all the ease went out of the afternoon. We went on chatting as if it hadn't, and presently had tea in the garden, and afterwards we went for a short walk through the woods behind the house. But Peter walked some distance ahead of his mother and me, with Jess at his heels, and Dr. Lindsay became absent-minded and forgot to finish a sentence she started to say to me and I began to wish that it was time for Owen and Margaret Loader to arrive, so that I should know what I was up against.

They came in the Jaguar, only a little while after we had returned from our walk.

Owen Loader was about forty, a tall man, well-built, with a rather large square head and a ruddy, good-humoured face with a small nose squashed almost flat against it. He had pale grey eyes and sun-bleached hair, which had receded from his temples, leaving only a downy, straw-coloured tuft above a forehead dotted with large freckles. He looked far more of a farmer than an author. A rich farmer too. I am not sure what there was about him that made me certain straight away that he was rich. Perhaps I had already heard it somewhere, for I had heard of him, although I had never read any of his books. They were mainly about farming and country life and had a fair reputation. But there hadn't been so many of them, and they hadn't been such immoderate successes, that it could have been through them that he had achieved his air of opulence.

Margaret had it too, but it was easier in her case, to see where that look of wealth came from, than in her husband's. A small, dark woman with a little, pale, pointed face, as sad and still as a clown's and with a clown's provoking charm in its immobility, she was wearing a sleeveless, cream-coloured cotton dress that would have cost me a month's salary; her short dark hair had the sculptured look that comes only from constant and expensive attention, and she was wearing a ring with a diamond in it too large and a necklace of pearls too small to be anything but real.

In a low, diffident voice she told me how glad she was

to meet Peter's wife, as she and Peter were such very old friends, though she didn't suppose that he had thought of mentioning the fact.

" Peter's single-minded," she said with a soft laugh. " He can only think of one thing at a time." And turning to Peter, she put a hand on his shoulder in a light caress, then she turned to Dr. Lindsay and started to chatter about the reviews of her husband's last book, about her anger over one in *The Times Literary Supplement* and her joy over one in *The New Yorker*.

We were having our drinks indoors, in the big, shabby, comfortable sitting-room, because it became too cool in the garden to go on sitting there.

Owen Loader asked me how long Peter and I were staying with Dr. Lindsay and said that he hoped our visit wasn't to be a short one.

" I'm afraid it's hardly a visit at all," I said. " We've got to go back to London this evening."

" Oh, that isn't fair, Peter! " Margaret exclaimed. " I thought you'd come to stay."

" Another time," Peter said. I think they were the first words that he had said since Margaret had come into the room, and he avoided her gaze even now. " Anne's a working woman, you know."

" But I was going to ask you to dinner to-morrow," Margaret said. " To-night I can't, of course, because we're on our way over to Owen's mother, whom we always visit on a Sunday evening, unless we can think of an awfully good excuse. I mean, unless *I* can think of an awfully good excuse. Owen doesn't even try, he likes going there. Well, we'll have to arrange it for next time. When are you coming again? "

" I don't know." Peter's gaze went to Jess, who peeped in at the door to take a distrustful look at the Loaders. " As a matter of fact, I've got involved in something. I may be busy."

" But your job hasn't started yet, has it? " Margaret said. " I thought it didn't start till October."

" This has nothing to do with my job. I'm thinking of doing a bit of detective work."

" I suppose that means something to do with historical research," Owen said. " It's all a sort of detective work, isn't it? Have you stumbled on something particularly exciting, Peter? "

" No, this isn't history," Peter said. " Anne and I made the discovery this morning that I've got a double. He's so like me that Anne actually mistook him for me. And I think it would be interesting to track him down and find out who he is."

Margaret and Owen both gave exclamations of interest. Dr. Lindsay frowned, looked at Peter, then at me, then with concentration at the glass of sherry in her hand.

" This is the first I've heard about it," she said dryly.

" Well, I've been thinking it over, ever since it happened, wondering what to do," Peter said. " I wasn't sure if I really wanted to do anything about it."

" And now you've decided you do? " she said.

" I think so."

" You wouldn't listen to advice from me? "

He gave a non-committal smile. " Tell them what happened, Anne," he said. " You're the one who saw him."

" Just a minute," Dr. Lindsay said. " Do you mean you didn't see him yourself, Peter? "

" Only with a helmet on, getting on to a motor-bike."

" I see." She turned and shot one of her sharp questions at me. " What happened, Anne? "

" It was in a pub called the White Horse," I began, " the other side of Lachester——"

" Ah yes," Margaret murmured, " we know it. We go there sometimes too."

"Well, we'd stopped for petrol," I said and went on and told them the rest of it.

When I finished, Peter went round with the decanter, refilling our glasses. He was being very careful to keep his non-committal smile, to look as if he were entirely ready to be swayed by reason.

"Well now, I'm waiting for the advice," he said. "Go ahead." He looked at Dr. Lindsay.

But it was Owen, his eyes on her troubled face, who spoke first. "If I were you, Peter, I'd let it go at that. A double's just an accident of nature. And you've no particular use for one, have you? I mean, you aren't a famous figure who wants a stand-in when there's liable to be shooting, or anything of that sort."

"Only suppose he's my twin brother," Peter said. "You see—something you and Margaret don't know. I did have one. And isn't it natural for me to want to know whether he is or not?"

Dr. Lindsay put down her glass and folded her strong, square hands on her lap. "Now that this has happened, I think there's probably nothing for you to do but find out what you can for yourself," she said.

"You don't mind?" he asked.

"That's neither here nor there," she said. "The fact is, I don't think you're capable of leaving things as they are, so there'd be no point in suggesting it."

"But you'd sooner I left them—isn't that what you're saying?"

"Much sooner, but that's my own affair."

"I don't think I understand," he said. "If he's my brother . . ."

"It's *because* he may be your brother," she said. "Because you may find that blood's thicker than water. And what do you really know about this blood of yours?"

Peter's usually mobile face went curiously blank.

"Are you afraid it may be bad blood?"

"I don't mean that at all, as you really know quite well," she said. "I'm afraid simply that your feeling for this—this complete stranger, whose upbringing and environment have almost certainly been completely different from yours, and yet whom you're bound to feel is somehow very close to you, is likely to lead to—well, to nothing very satisfactory for either of you."

"And what about you, Anne?" he asked me. "What do you think?"

Before I could answer, Margaret said, in her soft, eager voice, "Oh, I'd look for him, Peter! You bet I would! Only how are you going to set about it? Advertise? Hire detectives?"

"As I've said already," Owen Loader said, "I'd keep clear of the whole thing. Forget it. Dr. Lindsay's absolutely right. It's always tempting to sentimentalise this family business, but it's damned stupid to act on it."

"Anne?" Peter insisted softly.

I shook my head. "I don't know, Peter."

"I'll do whatever you say."

I didn't believe him, and it didn't even please me much that he'd said it.

"I expect you'll look for him, whatever anyone says," I said.

Margaret gave one of the tiny smiles that barely affected the stillness of her face and yet seemed to light it up with an amazing amount of expression. Its expression now was of tender, sad, derision. Reaching out a hand to Peter, she lightly stroked the back of his neck with one finger.

"We all think you're such a stubborn mule, darling, it's no good giving you advice," she said. "You mild, quiet people, there's nothing on earth you'll stick at to get your own way. It's the big, solid, tough people like Owen who sometimes aren't afraid of giving way to other people and who sometimes—just sometimes, bless them!—are ready to do what one asks them."

Peter jerked sharply away from her caressing finger. He stood up, muttered something about wondering what had happened to Jess, although she was there in the room with us, and went out. As he went I saw the flash of some intense emotion in Margaret's eyes.

Afraid of letting her know that I had seen it, I turned my head away and caught Owen Loader watching me. There was a kind but detached interest in his glance, and a sort of regretful sympathy.

As I've said before, I know my state of mind at that time wasn't normal. In the dream in which I had been going round for the last month, I hadn't minded the fact that I knew hardly anything about Peter. In fact, there had been a peculiar delight in this lack of knowledge, for against this hazy background his image had had a vividness which had put him apart from anyone I had ever known before. And there had been satisfied vanity for me too in having been able to evoke love so quickly. But now, with Owen's eyes on my face, making me shrink from him as if his understanding were intended to hurt me, I suddenly began to feel as if I were on a steep slope, with my foothold beginning to slip from under me.

CHAPTER III

PETER DID NOT reappear until some time after the Loaders had left, which fortunately they did a few minutes later, with Margaret complaining resignedly, as Owen manœuvred her to the car, of having to spend the rest of the evening with a deaf old woman. There was an absent-minded sort of humour in her complaining, to which Owen responded with an equally vague smile.

It was as if her reluctance to visit her mother-in-law were an old, established joke between them, which didn't amuse either of them as much as usual this evening. Margaret kept looking around her with the blank, appealing sadness of her clown's face altered to something that looked remarkably like real unhappiness. If she was looking for Peter, she was disappointed.

He returned at last when Dr. Lindsay called him to the cold supper that Mrs. Joy had left ready in the dining-room. Half-way through this meal, the telephone rang and Dr. Lindsay had to take her bag, get out her car and go to a patient whose baby was arriving a week early. So it was very much earlier than we had intended that Peter and I started back to London.

For a time we had nothing to say to each other. I couldn't stop thinking about Margaret and yet I couldn't bring myself to say a single thing about her. Because of the tension in Peter's face, I thought that he must be thinking about her too, and about the leftovers of the relationship between them, whatever it had been, and of which, so far, I had been told nothing. But as we reached the roundabout before the White Horse, and as if we had been in the middle of a discussion, he said thoughtfully, " Anyway, there's one thing I can do straight away. I can call in here and leave our address with them."

I roused myself then out of my own preoccupation to answer, " But if they hadn't seen him before, there's no reason to expect him to come back, is there? "

" If he did come back, though, they'd remember him," Peter said, steering us into the car-park.

I had an impulse to start a quarrel with him, reminding him that he'd promised to do whatever I wanted about looking for his double, and that he hadn't yet troubled to find out what I wanted. But the quarrel wouldn't really have been about the double.

Yawning, I said, " All right, go ahead."

" Aren't you coming in with me? "

" What good would that do? "

" Suppose he's there, don't you want to see him? "

" All right," I said, " but I don't imagine you'll find him as easily as that."

I got out of the car and we edged our way towards the corkscrew pillars of the portico, between an old Ford and the van belong to Geo. Biggs, which was still where it had been in the morning.

Inside, the heavy scent of the floor-polish was almost lost in the smell of tobacco-smoke and human beings. The place was crowded. But it took us only a moment to make certain that the man we wanted wasn't there. However, Mr. Biggs was there, in the same corner as before, in the same brown overall, with his hat on his head and an elbow on the bar and a hand folded around another double whisky.

" Look who's here! " he shouted, seeing Peter. " If it isn't Albert! "

Several people turned to look at us, including Mr. Galpin, the landlord, who gave a swift glance at us working our way through the crowd towards Mr. Biggs, then turned back to the beer-pump.

Mr. Biggs caught Peter by the shoulder and held on to it hard, as if he wanted to be certain that he was real.

" Albert himself," he declared thickly, his eyes focusing uncertainly on Peter's face, " come back to vindicate what I've been telling you, my friends. Two of 'em, it's the literal truth. And this is my old friend, Albert."

There were grins on several of the faces near us.

A woman who was helping Mr. Galpin behind the bar, said, " Now, George, we've heard all about it quite often enough this evening."

She was thin, sharp-featured and middle-aged, with the skin drawn in tight, dry wrinkles over the bones of her face and her grey hair waved in small, tight ridges. There was an air of forced geniality about her, covering weariness and irritability.

Mr. Biggs gave her a truculent stare.

"Please take note of the fact, Mrs. Galpin," he said, speaking with great distinctness, "this is my old friend Albert. And Albert would like something to drink, if it isn't troubling you too much. What'll it be, Albert?"

"I'm sorry, I'm not Albert," Peter said. "I'm the other one. But I'd like very much to find Albert, so I'd be extremely grateful if you'd tell me the rest of his name and where he lives."

"Albert," Mr. Biggs repeated positively. "If you doubt me, I can get a friend of mine to vouch for the truth of every word I've said—a Member of Parliament and an educated man of the highest reputation—he'll back me up, dear old fellow. Dear old boy."

Mrs. Galpin turned away and whispered to her husband and he came to Peter's rescue.

"I'm sorry, sir, you won't get very much sense out of him at this time of the evening," he said. "Is there anything I can do for you?"

Mr. Biggs leant heavily on Peter's shoulder. "Don't listen to him, boy," he said confidingly. "I'm the one who can tell you things. All kinds of things. For instance, I can tell you about when I was in the East, the Far East——"

"The very Far East," somebody interrupted.

"It's the truth!" Mr. Biggs shouted furiously. "I can tell you most 'straordinary things that happend to me in the East. Didn't you ever hear of the great Rajah Biggs?"

Several voices answered, egging him on. Frowning with displeasure at what was happening in his shiny, polished bar-room, Mr. Galpin caught Peter's eye and gestured to him to move farther along, so that he could talk to

B

him. Peter managed to disengage his shoulder from Mr. Biggs's grip and followed.

"I'm looking for the man who was in here this morning," he said, "the one I'm supposed to look so like."

"Ah yes. But as I told you then, I don't remember him coming in here before, so I can't tell you anything about him."

"Yet Mr. Biggs seems to know him," Peter said.

"Because he called him Albert? That's a name he gives to anyone he sees around this time of the evening, I couldn't tell you why."

"Well, if this man came in again, you'd recognise him, wouldn't you?"

"Oh yes, I'd certainly do that."

"If he does . . ." Peter took a notebook out of his pocket, tore a sheet out of it, wrote on it and held it out. "If he does, would you have the kindness to give him this? I'm curious about him and I'd like to get in touch with him."

Dubiously Mr. Galpin took the piece of paper, glanced at it and tucked it under a bottle on one of the shelves behind him.

"I'll do my best," he said, "but as I said, I don't think he's been in here before and there's no special reason to expect him back."

Moving up beside him, Mrs. Galpin said, "Oh, I remember him, Arthur. Not in here, but I've seen him several times in Lachester with that pretty dark-haired girl who used to edit the woman's page on the Lachester Herald before she married that writer. . . ." Her voice faded. Swiftly her tired gaze went from Peter's face to mine. Then she turned away mumbling, "Oh, I may be wrong—I dare say I'm wrong."

It made me want to laugh, but it also started a prickling feeling of anger inside me, which, as we drove off again into the deepening dusk, made me say viciously, " Since things have happened as they have, Peter, hadn't you better tell me all about Margaret? Things are getting embarrassing."

He didn't answer for so long that I thought he wasn't going to answer at all. But at last he said, " All right, though why it's got to be done when the whole damn' thing's over ... It *is* over, you know, about as completely as it could be."

" Does Margaret think so? "

" Margaret? " He gave a chilly little laugh. " Margaret stopped it. She killed it very successfully in one short, sharp talk about the virtues of marrying a man who was kind and understanding and just happened to have a lot of money."

" Were you engaged to her, then? "

" So I thought. . . . Hell, why did we have to start this? It does a horrible thing to me. I start feeling a sick sort of anger, which nothing else makes me feel. It's like swallowing something that gets stuck. You retch helplessly and you don't know what's going to happen next. And it's all pride. That's all—not love, if that what's worrying you. It's having had to swallow my own damned pride and do it with my usual charming smile too, because everyone else felt that would make it easier. Not perhaps for me, but for everyone else."

He drew a long breath, peering ahead into the uncertain light in which solid forms looked like shadows and shadows seemed to have living substance and the headlights of the car only increased their treacherous mingling with one another. " It seemed I was deficient all along the line," he went on, " I was hard as nails. I thought only of myself. I wasn't reliable—or quite normal, on account of my abnormal history. . . . So there you are, that's all the story that needs telling. You don't want to be told all the dreary details, do you? Just what's been left behind of it all, isn't that what matters? If any of it does."

After a moment I said, " No, I don't suppose it does matter. But, Peter——"

" What? "

I'm not sure what I had been about to say. I was gazing blindly at the lights flicking past us and thinking that he ought to have ended by telling me that he loved me. But perhaps it's a difficult thing to do, when you are driving too fast in busy Sunday evening traffic. Or perhaps he was waiting for me to do it first.

I might have tried, if I hadn't started to feel a little sick and dizzy as I started to wonder if by any chance I had simply been the sacrifice that he had made to his hurt pride, his revenge on Margaret, who perhaps still meant far more to him, whether in love or in bitterness, than I did. Anyway, there no longer seemed to be any point in saying whatever I had meant to say.

Instead, I said, " That abnormal history of yours—won't you ever be able to forget it? "

" At the moment that would be a bit difficult wouldn't it ? " he said.

And that was all that either of us said for a long time.

It was about eleven o'clock when we reached our home. We were living in a flat in a block in Belsize Park, where I had lived on my own for two years, having been lucky enough to find it soon after coming to London from a Dorset village, to look for a job after my mother's death. The flat consisted of a big bed-sitting-room, a bathroom and a minute kitchen. When we married, Peter had moved into it from lodgings in West Kensington and though we had talked of looking for a larger flat, we hadn't yet found the effort worth our while.

I slept badly that night because I couldn't stop thinking about Margaret and trying to puzzle out what her existence and the effect that she had on Peter ought to mean to me. What I had on my mind was something more complex than jealousy. It was a great dread that I had missed the real meaning of everything that had happened to me during the last month and that that nightmarish idea that I had had in the car was the truth, a truth which Peter himself perhaps didn't know yet, but which he would soon recognise if he saw any more of Margaret.

Well, the sooner the better, if that was how it was. But suppose it wasn't? And how was I to know if it was or not?

My mind swung wearily from one belief to the other, from dread to confidence and back again, and somewhere in the middle of it I discovered a sharp and frightening distrust of my own feelings. What was this marriage that I had rushed into on a blind, enchanted impulse? I had met a man on a holiday. Each of us had been with friends. We had all gone about together; we had walked, had swum in mountain lakes and seen the sights. And then he and I had gone away one day and got married. And it had taken me only until to-day, until my first encounter with a chance few of the realities of the life that he had lived before he knew me, to start wondering how any of this could ever have come about and to start struggling out of the dream.

Next day, for the first time since I had met Peter, I was glad that I had to go out to my job. The firm I worked for had offices in Gray's Inn and in the sheer familiarity of the place and the people I had been working amongst for three years, there was something that steadied me and gave me back some of the self-confidence that had been chipped away during the night. I suddenly realised that I had no intention of giving notice for some time, although only the day before, on the way down to Lachester, I had been thinking that it would be a pleasant thing to do.

But when I left the office at half-past five and found Peter waiting for me on a bench in one of the green courtyards, as he had done several times during the last week or two, the pendulum swung violently in the other direction. The mere sight of him there gave me the same reassurance as it had when he appeared, the Peter I knew, after I had been staring in horror at his double in the pub. As I sat down beside him and as we talked about what to do that evening, deciding to have dinner in a small Soho restaurant to which we had developed a certain attachment, then go on to a cinema, I felt as dizzy from the sudden rush to my head and heart of my trust in him as I had from its ebbing away.

But Peter turned out to be in an abstracted mood and I soon began to feel a chilling conviction that he had come to meet me because he hadn't wanted to spend an evening at home, with the risk hanging over him all the time that I might start talking about Margaret again.

We did start talking about her again presently, but that was because we bought an evening paper in Holborn and when we had reached the restaurant Peter opened it to read the names of the current films and saw something else which made him exclaim, " Good lord! "

Thrusting the paper at me across the table, he said, " Look at that! "

He was pointing at a small paragraph near the foot of the front page. Reading it, I learnt that on the previous evening a house called Long Grange, near Lachester, the home of Mr. and Mrs. Owen Loader, had been broken into while they were out for the evening and jewellery worth five thousand pounds had been stolen.

" Five thousand pounds! " I exclaimed. I was not in a mood to feel sympathetic to Margaret Loader. " You know, I can't even imagine what it feels like to own, let alone lose, jewellery worth five thousand pounds."

" I expect it was insured," Peter said. " All the same, it must feel pretty horrible."

" Yes," I agreed. " The enemy coming into one's home. . . ."

" They went out every Sunday evening to see Owen's mother, and I suppose the burglar knew that," Peter said, " And that can't be a pleasant thought, that someone who knows you well enough to know a thing like that has handed on the information."

" Only it could have been done unintentionally, just gossip in the hearing of the burglar, or some friend of the burglar's," I said.

We went on talking about the burglary over dinner. Afterwards we went to see a film which turned out to be about a bank-robbery. So it wasn't surprising that the subject was still on our minds when we reached home. As we went up the stairs to the flat, Peter was saying that he thought he would ring his mother up to ask her if she knew anything about how it had happened. And when someone who had been waiting furtively in the shadows of the landing outside our door moved suddenly forward to intercept us, I clutched at Peter's arm in a sudden panic that the enemy had come to our home too.

CHAPTER IV

THE BEATING of my heart returned to normal as I realised that it was a girl who stood there, the girl whom I had seen the day before in the White Horse.

She stared at Peter. She looked just as she had the day before, red tea-cosy of hair, cotton waterproof and long, pale legs. She gave an incredulous whistle.

" Steady," Peter said. " I'm real. I'm not going to fade away through the wall.

" Well, if I hadn't been warned . . . ! " Her greenish eyes gleamed in their dark hollows of mascara. " I suppose you *aren't* Tom. You aren't just putting something over on me? Because if you are . . . No, Tom's thinner than you are and he's got a pimple on his chin. I noticed it this morning. You aren't Tom. But who are you, then? "

Peter had got out his latchkey.

" Let's go in and talk it over," he said.

But she was in the way, between us and the door. She turned her white face to give me a flat stare.

" You're the girl who was in that pub yesterday, trying to get off with Tom," she said.

" A case of mistaken identity—I'm sure you can understand it now," I said.

" That's right," she said. " Tom said he'd done nothing himself, he said it was all you. I didn't believe him, but it looks like it was the truth for once."

" I thought his name was Albert," Peter said.

" Albert? Oh, I know what you mean. You heard that drunk in the pub calling him Albert. He calls everyone Albert. No, his name's Tom. Tom Hearn. What's yours? "

" Peter——" He hesitated. " Lindsay. Now suppose we go inside and talk it all over in comfort."

" Well, I don't mind—I dare say it's all right," she said dubiously and moved aside to let him get at the door.

Peter unlocked it and I went in first leading the way into the bed-sitting-room. It was, as I've said, a fairly big room, with a bed and some built-in cupboards in an alcove, which had a curtain to draw across it and cut it off from the rest of the room. But we didn't often draw the curtain, because the room felt airier and brighter without it.

I saw the girl take a thoughtful look round at the two comfortable chairs, the small mahogany writing-desk,

the bookcase, the table, which had a lot of Peter's papers
spread out over it, and the two bright rugs, which had
been my main extravagance in furnishing the room. She
seemed to be trying to deduce all she could about the
situation in which she found herself before committing
herself to coming more than a couple of steps inside.

Peter opened the cupboard in which we kept our sherry.
" Why did Tom send you, instead of coming himself? "
he asked.

" He didn't—Mum sent me," the girl said. " Tom
said, ' Don't you do anything about it, Sandra, I want no
part of it,' he said. But Mum said if one of us didn't come
and see what it was about, she'd come herself. And Mum's
got no sense to speak of, so I came, that's all."

" Sandra? " Peter said, taking the cork out of the
bottle. " Sandra what? "

" Hearn," she said.

" You're——" He hesitated as he was about to pour
out the drinks. " You're Tom's wife? "

" Wife! " she said contemptuously. " When I marry,
it's going to be a man who doesn't blow all his pay on
drink and motor-bikes. I'm his sister."

Peter's hand jerked and some sherry went on to the
polished table. He straightened up.

" You're Tom's sister. And—Mum? "

I could see the effort he had to make to keep his voice
level.

" She's our mother, of course."

" What's her name? "

" Ada Hearn."

Peter put down the bottle. He did it very carefully, as
if he were afraid that it would topple over on to the
floor. He gave himself a moment, then said quietly,
" I suspect you really know a lot more than I do about
all this, Sandra. We're brother and sister, aren't we? "

She came a reluctant step farther into the room and,

perching on the arm of an easy-chair, gave him a long,
penetrating stare.

"You said your name was Lindsay," she said. "So
I thought it was just chance, sort of, you and Tom
looking so alike."

"That's the name of the people who adopted me," he
said. "I've always gone by it. But my own name's
Hearn and my mother's name was Ada."

"Well," she said, "imagine that."

It was said with almost no feeling, but the first smile
that I had seen on her face momentarily softened the
line of her purple-tinted mouth. Then suddenly she
went into peals of laughter.

It gave Peter a shock. Then he started laughing too
and, picking up the sherry bottle again, filled three
glasses.

"Well, here's to a reunited family," he said.

But Sandra, who had slid down into the chair on the
arm of which she had been sitting, took no notice of the
glass that he had put in front of her, but went on laughing.

Peter gave me a quick glance. I shrugged my shoulders
and picked up my own glass. That drink was one that
I needed badly.

"A reunited family," Peter repeated. "I must arrange
to meet my mother and brother, Sandra."

Her laughter stopped with a little strangling cough.
She gave her thin body a wriggle, sat straight in the chair,
flattened her skirt over her kneecaps and picked up her
glass.

"Sorry," she said. "Really I'm sorry. I won't do
that again. It's just that it suddenly got into me . . . I
mean to say! . . . And Mum never being quite sure she
wants to admit Tom's her son, because she says she looks
too young to have a son that old. And now there'll be
two of you! Oh well, she'll get used to it. She's good at
getting used to things, Mum is."

With this enigmatic comment, she gave Peter and me a fleeting grin and drank most of her sherry.

Peter, as far as I could see, had recovered himself and had begun to enjoy the situation. Being good at getting used to things seemed to run in the Hearn family.

" Well, what do we do next? " he asked. " What about going round to see Mum and Tom this evening? "

" Oh, not this evening! " Sandra said quickly. " Tom's away and Mum's working."

" Working? "

" That's right. She's a hotel receptionist. She's on the evening shift just now."

" Couldn't we go to see her there then? "

" Not on your life—she'd be mad! They don't like your family coming around there. No, let me see . . ." She narrowed her greenish eyes at the glass that she was holding, swirling around the sherry that was left in it. " To-morrow. To-morrow afternoon. Tom'll be back then. He drives a lorry and he went up north this morning, but he'll be back by to-morrow afternoon."

" To-morrow afternoon then," Peter agreed, " though it seems a long time to wait."

" The fact is, I wouldn't really want to do anything till Tom's back," Sandra said. " The last thing he said was, ' You keep out of it, Sandra.' So you see what I mean—though Mum wouldn't want to wait. But it'll be better like that, see."

" I see," Peter said. " All right then, I'll come to-morrow afternoon."

" *We'll* come to-morrow afternoon," I corrected him, " and not before about five-thirty, because I don't think I can get away from the office before then."

Peter gave me a quick glance, then asked the girl: " Where do you live? "

She gave him an address which she said was a flat in a mews near Baker Street and Peter wrote it

down. She then started to ask him questions about where
he'd grown up and the people who'd adopted him and
what his job was and what he'd been doing yesterday
in the pub in Lachester. He wasn't expansive in his
answers; indeed, it struck me that he was telling her as
little as he could without actually refusing to answer, and
after a little while she gave him up and started on me.

Immediately I was afflicted by a feeling that I didn't
want this girl and her family to know any more about me
than I could help. I don't mean that there was any
particular thing that I wanted to hide from them. It
was simply an attack of that rather primitive fear that
knowledge of oneself in the hands of others is power.
And yet, in the circumstances, Sandra Hearn's curiosity
was normal, and she didn't seem to mind talking about
herself. She told us that she worked in the beauty
department of an Oxford Street store, was just learning the
job, but didn't know if she'd stick to it. All the same, it
was useful to have a trade, because you never knew. She
didn't want to get landed the way her mother had.

But as if she felt that her mother's life was a delicate
subject, she paused at that point, then said she ought to
be getting home. Peter offered to drive her there, but
she said no-thank-you very quickly and firmly.

He saw her down the stairs, however, and while he was
out of the flat, I had a sudden idea. I couldn't see the
street from any of my windows, but I could from a window
on the staircase. So as soon as the sound of Sandra's heels
on the concrete steps had faded out, I slipped out of the
flat and went to the window on the half-landing. From
there, after a moment, I saw her emerge on to the pavement and go walking quickly away up the street. But
she didn't go towards the tube-station, she went in the
opposite direction, disappearing at the first turning.

I waited, and after a moment I saw a motor-cycle
emerge from the turning and go down the hill towards

Chalk Farm. The man driving had a helmet on and might have been anybody, but even by the light of the street-lamps it was certain that the girl on the pillion behind him was Sandra.

Peter had just reached the landing and he saw them too. He laughed, then we went up the few stairs to the flat together, shut the door and he poured out more sherry.

" I've been a fool, haven't I ?—and you all warned me," he said. He laughed again and drank. " Well—here's to crime! "

" There's nothing actually criminal about saying Tom was away, driving his lorry, when he was really waiting round the corner," I said. " It's quite natural to want to take a rather careful look at you before getting involved. And in a way I rather liked her."

" Oh, so did I. Have you noticed how easy it usually is to like people who lie really fluently? "

" But it wasn't a very serious lie," I said.

" What——? Oh, about Tom being away—no, that wasn't serious."

" What other lie did she tell? "

" I'm inclined to wonder what, if anything, that she told us was true."

" What makes you think that? " I asked, looking at him curiously.

" Oh—just a feeling," he said.

I didn't believe that that was all it was, but when I tried to find out what was behind the feeling, he stopped me by saying that he was going to ring up his mother to find out what she knew about the Loaders' burglary.

He got through to Dr. Lindsay easily and they talked for a few minutes. When he rang off he told me, " It was quite a classy burglary. There was nothing crude about it, like smashing locks or windows. The thief obviously knew they'd be out for the whole evening and took his time. He climbed up the side of the house, got in at the bathroom window, which they hadn't fastened, opened their safe about as easily as you would a refrigerator and got away with everything inside. Margaret's lost everything she had except the pearls and the ring she was wearing yesterday. But it's all insured, so she isn't as desolated as she might be and Mother says she's bravely beginning to see the bright side. All the same, it seems to have been a nasty shock. Anne, about to-morrow . . ."

" I know," I said, " You don't want me to come."

" I was going to suggest it might be a good idea to let me prospect on my own," he said. " But you're set on coming are you? "

" Set like concrete."

" I see. Well, all right. I'll pick you up at the office."

We arranged that he would wait for me on the usual bench.

All the same, next day, when we had driven from Gray's Inn to Baker Street and had parked the car, I felt certain that Peter had done at least a little prospecting on his own already, for he showed no hesitation in looking for the right turning out of Baker Street and he found the not very conspicuous entrance to the mews without having to search for it.

The mews was a quiet-looking place. Indeed, with its cobbles and tiny houses, some with brightly painted doors and gay window boxes, it had a misleading air of being a little street in an old village. Pinned to a door painted lilac was a card with the name Hearn on it. As Peter rang the bell, I pointed out to him that the card was a new one and that the ink hadn't yet begun to fade.

" They can't have been here long," I said.

" Perhaps not—on the other hand, perhaps they've just put up a nice new card to impress us," he suggested.

" Wouldn't that be an odd thing to do? "

" Awfully odd. I think we may run into several odd things, Anne. But will you do something for me?—don't notice anything odd. We'll talk about it afterwards."

" But——" I began.

The door opened and Tom Hearn stood there.

For the first time, so far as I knew, he and Peter looked at one another. For the first time I saw them together. They were even more alike than I remembered, and more alike, I thought, than either had expected. Tom looked even more like Peter than he had on the Sunday before because instead of the red pullover and flannels, he was in a grey suit not unlike Peter's and he had had a haircut. And for the moment the expressions on their two thin faces, with the high foreheads and the brown eyes with the little wrinkles fanning out from the corners, was the same.

Both faces had gone curiously still as each looked into this living mirror. Then Tom thrust out a hand.

" Well, well! " he said with forced heartiness. " The wanderer's come home, eh? Pleased to meet you, brother. Welcome and all that."

Peter hesitated, then said, " Thank you," in a subdued tone.

I thought that his brother's appearance had taken him by surprise and that he was more moved than he had been prepared for.

" This is Anne," he went on quickly, as if he wanted to avoid all further talk of the strangeness of that meeting.

Tom thrust out a hand to me, looking me up and down with a broad smile.

" We've met before, Anne," he said. " Afraid I must've made a bad impression. But I wasn't really as bad as I looked. I'd been out all night with the lorry, coming down from the north, and I was tired, just plain tired. When I'm like that a single drink does for me. Matter of fact, I didn't want to go out at all that day, but Sandra'd set her heart on a day by the sea. That's what we did after you saw us—went on another fifty miles, then spent the afternoon sleeping on the beach. Don't ask me the point of it. Well now, come upstairs and meet the old lady. She's in a bit of a state about meeting the wandering child, but you'll allow for that. You've got to make allowances in life, plenty of allowances."

He turned and led the way up the narrow little staircase.

At the top was Sandra, leaning against the jamb of an open door. She was wearing a tight black dress, her long black shoes with their dagger-like heels, and gilt bracelets as broad as handcuffs.

" Hallo," she said woodenly, her small face showing no expression at all as she moved languidly back into the room so that we could enter.

As we did so, a voice said sharply, " Oh God! "

From a chair by the fireplace a woman rose quickly and stood for an instant, staring incredulously at Peter. Then she moved swiftly forward and stood in front of him.

" Oh God! " she repeated very softly, gazing deeply into his face.

CHAPTER V

WHAT AMAZED ME most about Ada Hearn was how young she looked. If I hadn't known that it was impossible, I should have guessed that she was under forty. She was very slim and there was a bony sort of grace in her swift striding across the room. Her hair was fair and she wore it straight, falling to her shoulders, which helped to make her look young and artless. She did not wear much make-up and her dress was a simple flowered cotton. Her face was very like Sandra's, except that there was an unrestrained excitability in its expression. Her eyes, of the same greenish colour as Sandra's, shone with emotional brilliance as she gazed at Peter. Then she caught up one of his hands and drew it, all of a sudden, to her heart.

"Lord, how could I ever have done it?" she asked in a whisper.

"All right, Mum, no need to work yourself up about it," Tom said. "The lamb's come back to the fold—come in very good style too, so he isn't likely to start blaming you for anything, is he?"

"Peter——? Peter's a nice name," she went on softly. "Do you blame me for what I did, Peter?"

"Oh, Mum!" Sandra said.

"I did it for the best, Peter—I did it for you," Ada Hearn said.

Peter looked embarrassed, but also as if, in another moment, he might start laughing, which I didn't understand, unless it was from nervousness.

"Oh, it's all right, quite all right," he said in a staccato way.

As if disappointed that he hadn't responded with more emotion, Ada Hearn dropped his hand and turned to me.

"I'm a silly, all right," she said. "He probably doesn't even believe that I used to think about him. And of course he doesn't blame me, because I don't suppose he's given me a thought. He went to nice people, I took care of that—well-off people, too, who'd give him all the things I couldn't. His father . . . Well, he did his best for me, but we couldn't get married and so . . . Anyway he was killed in the war, poor old boy. Sandra doesn't even remember him, though Tom does—don't you, Tom? You remember what a fine old boy he was."

"Sure, sure," Tom said. "Now let's drop all that and have a drink—a drink to the return of the whatsit son—you know what I mean. The one who lived among swine. No offence meant to anyone."

" I should think not and we will not have a drink," his mother said sharply. " We're going to have a nice cup of tea. Sandra . . ."

Sandra gave a shrug of her shoulders and went out. I heard a tap turned on and the clatter of crockery in the kitchen.

As we all sat down and Tom handed round cigarettes, I looked round the room. It had one shiny pink wall, one black one and two in black and gold stripes. All were rather faded and the room was not very clean. It was impersonal too, as if the things that filled it, the pale, plywood furniture, the very uncomfortable little arm-chairs on which we were sitting and the lamps with shades like swelling blisters at the ends of doublejointed-fingers, had never, in all their rickety lives, been treasured. They might have been bought by catalogue after some hasty study of a furnishing magazine, been thought smart for a week and then forgotten.

While Sandra made the tea, Ada Hearn started to tell Peter about his father. She told him how young she had been and how ignorant and how madly in love she had fallen with the man of whom Peter and Tom were, she assured him, the spitting image. He had been in the Navy, but she was vague as to his ship and his rank, and said she preferred not to mention his name, because she'd never done a thing, all her life, to embarrass his family and she didn't mean to start now. He'd been away at sea when the twins were born and she hadn't felt certain that she would ever see him again, and that had been why, listening against her own instincts to the advice of well-meaning relations, she had let Peter be adopted.

" Afterwards, when he'd come back and I knew he was going to look after me as well as he could," she said, " I tried to get you back, but it was too late, they told me. I'd signed something and there was nothing to be done about it. Anyway, they said, it wouldn't be fair on the other people, the ones who'd got you, and of course I understood that. You were a lovely baby, dear, and I expect it would have broken that other woman's heart to give you up. You were both lovely babies, you and Tom."

She sighed, her green eyes growing moist with tenderness.

Tom gave a snort of laughter, which made Sandra, who came in just then, turn on him with a scowl.

" All right, all right," he said to her defensively. " I know Mum's got to have her big scene. But she's embarrassing the feller. He won't come again if she keeps on telling him what he was like in nappies."

" As a matter of fact, I'm enormously interested," Peter said. " I've often wondered about my father. He was killed in the war, was he? "

Ada Hearn fetched another deep sigh. " That's right. You needn't be ashamed of him, Peter, you can be proud. As I'm sure he'd be proud of his two sons if he was here to see you now."

" And maybe of a whole lot more than us two, in all the other ports," Tom suggested.

" Tom! " his mother cried. " Don't you ever say a thing like that again. Your brother——" She gave a swift look at Peter. " Your brother would never say a thing like that. He's got nice feelings. It wouldn't do you any harm to take notice of that."

" There's nothing wrong with my feelings, it's just the company I keep," Tom said, catching my eye as he did so and giving me a wink.

" Well," Ada said, turning back to Peter, " you don't want to bother about Tom. He's always kidding. Now tell me about yourself, dear—and about your wife too. I can't help wondering how she's feeling about all this, I mean, finding out your real family are just people like us. She can't ever have expected it. Meeting you, I mean, she can't ever have expected a mother-in-law like me. But I tell you what, Mrs.—Mrs. Lindsay——"

"Call her Anne, like Peter and me do," Tom interrupted, with the grin that was so like Peter's and yet so different.

"Anne," Ada turned the force of her brilliant, emotional gaze on me. "I tell you what, Anne, you needn't ever be afraid of any of us, Tom or Sandra or me, getting in your way and making nuisances of ourselves. We aren't like that. It's wonderful for us to have found Peter again—looking at the two of them, I tell you my heart's so full, I hardly know how to contain myself— but it'll be for Peter to say if he wants to see us again. I'd never push in where I could be any embarrassment to him or to you either. So don't let any thought of that come between you."

"Poor Anne, got two mothers-in-law instead of one," Tom said. "You can't expect her to be raising a cheer, can you?"

Sandra whirled on him. "Can't you shut up for once?" she snarled. "What are you trying to do— spoil everything?"

"Sorry, sorry," Tom said. "I'm just trying to be my usual friendly self to all comers—even if I can't have a drink. But perhaps Pete and me can go out and have one together some time. Twin brothers ought to know each other. What about that, Pete?"

"Oh yes," Peter answered. "We must do that."

He said this quickly, as if he had been waiting for the suggestion, and he looked, I thought, as if he would have liked to act upon it at once. Unlike his brother, he was not attempting to be his usual friendly self. His quiet, wary politeness was quite unlike the behaviour that I had expected from him. Ada, I thought, had tried to generate emotion in him too quickly and had put him on guard.

She seemed to suspect this herself, for she did not repeat it. Pouring out the tea, she started to chat about herself. She told us about the hotel where she worked and about the different things she had done before she had drifted into the job. She had been a professional ballroom dancer once, but a fall had put a stop to that. She had been in a concert party. She had been a waitress. She had worked in shops.

"And considering I never had any training of any kind," she said, "except what I picked up as I went along, I do think I haven't done so badly. Now tell me, Peter, just what is it you do yourself? Sandra said you told her something about a university, but I can't say I understood really."

As if relieved to have something impersonal to talk about, Peter started to tell her a little about what it meant to be a member of a university department. A very little, even less than he had tried to tell me, and Ada Hearn nodded with grave blankness from time to time, her thick, blonde hair swinging forward as she did so, then being tossed back again with a movement so youthful that again I marvelled at the fact that she must be over forty. The hard life that she had described to us hadn't harmed her looks or vitality.

We stayed for about an hour. When we left, Tom saw us down the stairs and at the door repeated that he and Peter ought to go out on their own sometime.

"Without," he added, slipping an arm through mine and patting my hand, "the women."

"Yes," Peter said. "What about now, Tom?"

The suggestion took me by surprise and my first impulse was to protest, but I managed to say nothing. However, Tom also seemed startled and in some way put out.

"Sorry, no can do—not to-night," he said. "Taking out the girl-friend. Sorry. But I'll ring up later in the

week—what about that? Can't say which day yet. I'm
going up north again. But I'll ring you when I get back
—definitely. What's your number? "

Peter gave him our number and Tom wrote it down,
then held out his hand to say good-bye.

As Peter took it, there was another strange stillness
between the brothers, as there had been when they first
met. Each, looking into the face of the other, seemed to
be searching for himself there, or it might have been for
something more than himself. Suddenly Tom's cheeks
flushed and I thought he was going to speak again. His
lips parted to speak and something undecided and yet
eager appeared in his eyes. Peter waited. But Tom
thought better of it, jerked his hand away abruptly, gave
us a wave, a grin, turned back into the house and let the
door shut with a bang.

Peter and I walked back to the car.

As we started the drive homewards, Peter said, " And
what did you think of all that, Anne? "

" Well, they're your family," I said. " What did you
think of it? "

" It's a bit complicated," he answered. " There are
some things to explain first. You see, I went round there
this morning. I could have told you about that before
we went this afternoon, but I thought I'd wait until we'd
both seen them—all of them. I wanted us to make up
our minds separately whether or not we'd any doubts
about Tom—about whether there's any possibility at
all that he isn't my brother."

" I don't see how there can be," I said.

" We're really so alike? "

" Oh heavens, yes! Couldn't you see that yourself? "

" At first glance, yes," Peter said in a worried voice.
" It felt very queer and uncanny. But the longer I looked
at him, the more uncertain I seemed to feel about what
I looked like anyhow."

" That's natural," I said, " and even to me, he seems a little less like you than he did at first. All the same, the resemblance is staggering, and I don't think two people can be as alike as that without being twins."

" No," Peter said sombrely, " I don't think so either. And that creates a rather tricky situation."

" Wasn't it clear from the start it was going to be tricky? "

" Oh yes."

" But somehow it isn't what you expected," I said. " Your mother——"

" She isn't my mother, Anne," he said.

I thought for a moment that he had said this out of loyalty to Dr. Lindsay. But as I was wondering how to take it, he went on, " They're a stupid lot, not to have thought I'd probably know a certain amount about my mother. Perhaps Tom really doesn't. We don't know anything yet about how he grew up, and perhaps he never tried to find out about her. But I made an attempt to find her and though I never managed to trace her—I think she may have gone abroad—I got her birth certificate from Somerset House. And the truth about her is that she was thirty-three when Tom and I were born, and as I'm twenty-five, that would make her fifty-eight now. Well, could that woman we saw to-day be fifty-eight? "

" Heavens, no—that'd be quite impossible! " I said.

" I put her myself at about thirty-seven or -eight," Peter said, " perhaps just about old enough to be Sandra's mother."

" But if Sandra's your sister——"

" She isn't, if she's Ada's daughter—or rather, Ivy's daughter. Ivy May—I think that's her real name. And I think Sandra's her daughter all right, because they've got the same sort of eyes. So the question is, what were

they up to to-day? Why did they try to make me think
that the Mays are my mother and sister? "

"How did you find out that May is their name?"
I asked.

"It was this morning," he said. "Suddenly, after
you'd left for the office, I thought I'd go and take a look
at that mews and see what sort of place this family of
mine lived in. I was rather suspicious already, because
of that business of sending Sandra in to take a look at us
while Tom waited outside. I didn't know what it meant—
I still don't—but I didn't like it. So I went along and when
I was just outside that lilac-coloured door, I heard
someone coming downstairs, so I dodged back to the
entrance of the mews and I saw that woman come out
and walk away. Only she was dressed rather differently
from how she was when we saw her this afternoon.
There wasn't any homely simplicity about her. I could
see the flash of her fingernails half-way down the street.
But it didn't occur to me she'd turn out to be Ada Hearn.
I thought she was simply some friend of Sandra's. I
didn't want her to see me, because with my likeness to
Tom she might have guessed who I was and realised I
was doing a little snooping. So I waited for a bit then
I went back to the door."

"And you saw a card on it . . . ! " I was beginning to
understand.

"Yes," Peter said, "there was a card, but it didn't
have the name Hearn on it. The new card you noticed
went up since this morning. The name on the card
then was Mrs. Ivy May. Not that that, by itself, would
have meant anything sinister. It could have been a
landlady's name, or the name of an old tenant, which the
Hearns hadn't bothered to change. But while I was
wondering what to do next, an old crone looked out of
a window next door and shouted down to me that I'd
just missed my ma-in-law. Not my ma, you see. I started

to say, ' Oh, thank you very much,' when she gave me a stare as if I'd gone mad and slammed the window down."

" It was your voice," I said. " She thought you were Tom and probably thought you'd put on a different one to make fun of her. But Peter, I don't understand . . ."

" I don't either," he said.

" It looks as if Tom and Sandra are married, doesn't it? "

" Yes."

" I don't understand and I don't like it," I said. " Not one bit. But at least there's one thing—if they aren't your family, you needn't bother about them any more."

" Ah, but Tom is my family—you're sure of that yourself," he said.

" But if they're crooks, Peter . . ."

" Then it's all the more important that I should try to get to know Tom a little, isn't it? I want to see him by himself—without Ivy May, without Sandra. Because a twin brother is a person who gives one a feeling of responsibility. He's almost a part of oneself. It's a very queer thing to run into all of a sudden at my age, but there it is. So when he rings up, I'll meet him—definitely, as he said himself."

CHAPTER VI

IT WAS TWO DAYS before Peter heard from Tom. By then we had given him up for that week, and had arranged to go down to Lachester next day to spend the week-end with Dr. Lindsay. I was at the office when Tom telephoned, but Peter rang me up straight away to tell me of it, saying he had arranged to meet Tom that evening at a pub in Paddington.

I should have liked to go too, but I thought this was an occasion when I had better be careful not to get in the way, so when Peter had rung off, I began to consider the evening ahead, and thought that something I might do was pay a long overdue visit to some friends of mine, Daniel and Lucy Barfoot, who lived in Hendon.

They hadn't yet been told of my marriage, in fact, didn't even know of Peter's existence, and this, if they didn't hear of it soon, would give them a justifiable grievance. For they were very old friends, having been friends of my parents.

That friendship had been a somewhat stormy one, for Mr. Barfoot had been an inspector of schools when my father had been a young and progressive headmaster and the two of them had successfully failed to agree about almost everything. But Mr. Barfoot wouldn't have enjoyed it if he had found himself agreeing too often with anyone. Keeping up a reputation for irascible prejudices was one of his ways of adding to the interest of life.

His wife was a gentle, vague, silent woman, slightly lame, who appeared to live for her tiny garden and a pair of budgerigars and to be thankful to anyone who would take her husband off her hands for a time. When my mother died, two years after my father, and I had come to London, looking for a job, I had lived with the Barfoots until I had found my flat and had grown very fond of them. So to visit them and prepare them to meet Peter was becoming urgent. Telephoning Mrs. Barfoot, I was asked to supper that evening.

I went to Hendon straight from the office, without going home first. The Barfoots' house was semi-detached, with a touch of half-timbering and a gable or two and it was set behind a privet hedge and a row of red-leaved prunus. When I arrived, Mrs. Barfoot was in the garden, weeding around some hydrangeas. She waved her little hand-fork in greeting and told me to go in, as the door was open and Daniel was expecting me. Then she returned to her weeding, placidly forgetting my existence.

I went in and found Mr. Barfoot in the room which he called his study or his workshop, according to the mood that he was in. It had once been the dining-room of the neat little house, but the Barfoots had long ago settled down to the comforts of eating in the kitchen and Mr. Barfoot's belongings had been allowed to remain and multiply in this room.

He stood up when I came in and made vague, pleased noises at seeing me. At this time he was a little over seventy, but he would never admit this or let me know, on his birthday, just which birthday it was. He preferred to describe himself as too unbelievably ancient to remember, although this was always in the expectant tone of one who hopes to be contradicted. He was of medium height, thin and stoop-shouldered, with a face that had always reminded me, because of the long nose and flaring nostrils and the glassy, reckless glare of the eyes, of a rocking-horse that I had possessed in my childhood. The rocking-horse had been painted pale blue, with liver-coloured spots on it, and Mr. Barfoot's complexion resembled this in a modified way, because he had a bad digestion, which had given his skin a greyish pallor and his nose a slight purplish flush.

He fidgeted around me until I was settled in a chair with a cigarette alight, then he lit one for himself and sat down again. He was a very heavy smoker and the room, with its roll-top desk, bookcases, upright piano, lathe, carpenter's bench, and every shelf and table-top covered with strangely shaped pebbles and pieces of driftwood, mounted on wooden bases and always referred to by him as his sculptures, was thick with tobacco smoke.

"In case you're worrying about it," he said, "I think there's going to be a fish soufflé for supper. I put my foot down when Lucy said boiled fish with parsley

sauce. I said, ' Woman, can't you think of anything but
boiled fish with parsley sauce? There's chicken, for
instance,' I said, ' you know I can eat chicken! ' She
said we can't always be eating chicken, it's too expensive,
but what about a fish pie? ' Fish ! ' I said, ' Fish again! '
' Yes,' she said, ' the doctor said fish is the best thing for
you, but I'll make a fish soufflé for a change, if you like.'
So there you are, my dear, I did my best, though if you'll
be able to tell the difference between fish-pie and that
soufflé . . . Well, never mind. Now to what do we owe
the pleasure of this visit? Because, through the haze of
my own chatter, I can sense a certain impatience in you
to unburden yourself of something. What's the trouble? ''

I told him that I was married.

He exclaimed in amazement at the passing of time,
because I had been a child only yesterday, wrung my
hand, said some appropriate things and called Mrs.
Barfoot in to hear the news.

She said, " Well, that's very nice, my dear. I do hope
you'll both be very happy,'' and went back to her weeding.

Mr. Barfoot picked up one of his sculptures. It was a
large, flat pebble, which by accident was shaped like a
human face in profile. With a drill, he had given it one
round eye, which had given it a vacuously knowing
expression, and he had mounted it on a piece of ebony.
He communed with it thoughtfully for a moment, then
asked, " Would you care for this as a wedding-present? ''

" I shouldn't actually mind it," I said.

" All right," he said. " It's yours. Now go on. You've just
got married, and as dear Lucy says so adequately, that's
very nice. And yet you're a worried young woman. And
I suppose that's really why you're here, so go on and
talk.''

I did and found it a relief to do so.

I told him everything about Tom Hearn, Sandra and
Ivy. It all came out with more of a rush than I had

expected and I said more than I had ever intended, but that was something to which I was accustomed when I talked to Mr. Barfoot, for he was an insidiously good listener, interrupting just often enough, and shrugging and snorting a certain amount, because he was a fidget and couldn't simply have listened in silence, but saving up all important questions until he was sure that I had finished.

I didn't say much about Margaret Loader, but I told him what I knew of the burglary and to my surprise, because it was not a thing that I had meant to say, I ended up by saying that I was scared.

He asked me if I could say just what I was scared of and I said, " I suppose it's something in Peter's attitude. The truth is, of course, I really know him so little. But also, there's something creepy about this twin of his turning up like this. I don't like it. I don't like the feeling that they're together at this moment."

" You haven't by any chance been dreaming of white beads, have you? " Mr. Barfoot asked.

Now, as it happened, I had. The night after Peter and I had read of the Loaders' burglary, I had dreamt about a pearl necklace. The dream had been peculiarly upsetting and I had woken from it in a daze of fear and ever since I had felt a dread that I might dream it again. For the main thing that I remembered of it was the feeling of my own hands twisting a rope of pearls—huge pearls they had been in the dream—tight around somebody's neck. On waking, I had recognised quite calmly that the neck had probably been Margaret's, but that there was no need to suppose that this meant that I was actually getting ready to murder her. Yet the sense of guilty terror had remained, so Mr. Barfoot's insane, yet somehow entirely typical question seemed to arise out of knowledge so uncanny that I felt a prickle of cold up my spine.

" Dear, dear," he said, watching me intently. " It's

very bad luck for anyone connected with a twin to dream about white beads, you know. I must also warn you, if you've married a twin, you must never yield to the temptation to feed him on the flesh of iguana lizards."

"Well, I believe you really have gone quite mad at last!" I exclaimed. " I've never felt tempted to feed anyone on lizards."

" I don't expect they'd be any worse than boiled fish with parsley sauce," he said. " However, in Upper Guinea, I believe it is, there's a very firm ruling against feeding twins on iguana lizards. And, as I said, to dream of white beads is a portent of impending evil. But we're merely in the wilds of North London and not in Upper Guinea, so perhaps the same laws don't operate, and you may some day bring your Peter to eat here in reasonable safety. Now tell me, you haven't a sneaking belief, have you, that Peter's really known his brother for some time and engineered that remarkable meeting in the Lachester pub? "

Extremely startled, I exclaimed, " I never even thought of it! "

" No? " Mr. Barfoot said.

" Look," I said, " if you remember, I happen to have married him. I happen, you may be surprised to learn, to have quite a high regard for him."

" Now, now, don't take that tone with me, child," Mr. Barfoot said. " If it's common sense you're after, go and talk to Lucy. Talk bonemeal and compost. I thought you came to me for something more stimulating to the imagination. I'm only trying, if you'll give me the chance, to sort out exactly what's worrying you about these duplicate Peters. Not just the obvious reasons, but the real reason. Well, I'll believe you that it isn't the fear I suggested. Though if you've never even thought of it, perhaps you ought to start now. That meeting was either accidental, or it wasn't. A fifty-fifty chance, in fact."

" But what possible point could there have been in staging a scene like that? " I asked.

" What possible point can there have been in the scene you're quite sure the May woman and her offspring staged on Saturday? You know as much about the one as the other. There's obviously a plot of some sort. But I'm happy to say that I don't think you can be the intended victim of the plot. At most, you can only be a sort of stooge, who's going to come in useful sometime."

I felt rather offended at being brushed off as a stooge.

" How d'you know I'm not the victim? " I asked.

" You haven't enough money to be the victim of any plot," Mr. Barfoot said. " Now what about Peter himself? "

" Oh no."

" You mean, no money? "

" An assistant lecturer's salary, beginning in October."

" Ah. Scrub out Peter. What about Dr. Lindsay? "

" I don't know, but I don't think she can be specially well-off. Peter told me once she had to start her practice again when her husband died, to be able to bring Peter up."

" So the only rich people on the scene are their friends, the Loaders. And that reminds me, casting my mind back over the last month or two, I believe I've read of several jewel-thefts in that county."

" Well, what's that got to do with Peter, or Tom? "

" It was just a random thought," Mr. Barfoot said, picking up another of his pebbles and caressing it absently with the tips of his fingers. " But let's get back to what Ivy and Sandra are up to. Don't you think the likeliest thing is that Peter's likeness to Tom is to be used in some way—with or without Peter's knowing? Peter, for instance, could be seen around the place, while Tom was up to skulduggery of some sort. And they may have

felt they'd have more influence over Peter's actions if
he believed they were his mother and sister. I wonder if
they saw he hadn't swallowed that."

"I don't think so," I said. "I didn't myself until he
told me."

"But he may be telling Tom about it now."

"He may, I suppose."

"I rather hope he keeps it to himself," Mr. Barfoot
said. "Now have you anything else on your mind, apart
from the general uncanniness of twins? Because they are
uncanny, you know. That's been widely recognised in
most primitive societies. In some they're actually regarded
as visitations of the devil and the unfortunate mother and
children are sacrificed. And there's a general belief that
they're uncomfortably near to the animal kingdom—
that's because of the multiple birth, you see—and it's
necessary to perform complicated ceremonies or they
may turn back into monkeys."

"How do you happen to know such a lot about twins?"
I asked.

"I know a lot about all sorts of things," Mr. Barfoot
said, "which should dispose for ever of the superstition
that knowledge is power. What power have I? Barely
enough to say that it shan't be fish-pie. . . . Ah, here
comes Lucy, so prepare to meet your fate."

The door opened and Mrs. Barfoot limped in to fetch
us to supper in the kitchen.

The fish soufflé was very good, as I had known that it
would be, and Mr. Barfoot praised it without, apparently,
any memory of the dire things that he had prophesied,
while his wife, small and square, with her white hair
rolled up in a careless knot which as usual was half
undone, smiled placidly at his compliments out of the
impenetrably private world of her thoughts and listened
far more to her budgerigars in their cage above the sink
than to either her husband or me.

When supper was over, Mrs. Barfoot and I did the washing-up, while Mr. Barfoot made tea. This was done mostly in silence, but in the middle of it, Mrs. Barfoot suddenly said, " Daniel and I got married too after we'd known each other only a month, but of course that was war-time. All the same, everyone said we were foolish."

" So we were," Mr. Barfoot said. " Much better to look before you leap and so on."

" Much better," she agreed.

" But it's too late to tell Anne that." He put an arm round his wife's waist and gave her a kiss on the ear. " Anne's just chosen one of my sculptures as a wedding-present," so he said. " I'm flattered."

" Take no notice of him, dear," Mrs. Barfoot said. " You shall have something nice. I wonder what you'd like most. Silver? Linen? A motor-mower? "

This gave me a queer feeling, because I hadn't yet thought of my relationship to Peter as being one that would bring forth such substantial results. I said that perhaps I ought to talk it over with him before giving her an answer. I didn't think of doing it that evening, because I didn't expect to see him until quite late. But although I left the Barfoots early, knowing that they didn't like to sit up late, I found Peter already in the flat, islanded amongst his papers, and sombrely chewing a pencil. He looked irritable and moody and the moment I appeared, said with a disconcerted sort of anxiety, " Where've you been? "

" To see the Barfoots," I said. " I didn't expect you home so soon, or I'd have left a message."

" Who are the Barfoots? " he asked morosely, as if I had never mentioned them before.

" I've often told you about them," I said. " I thought you'd probably spend the whole evening with Tom."

" I can't remember you ever talking about any

c ˜

Barfoots," Peter said. " Why did you suddenly have to visit them to-night? "

" I've often talked about them," I repeated. " You didn't listen. Which would you soonest they gave us for a wedding-present, linen, silver or a motor-mower? "

" A motor-mower," he said.

" But we haven't got a lawn," I said.

" Well, one can always use a spare motor for something. Where do these wonderful friends of yours live? "

" I've told you before—Hendon. Your evening with Tom seems to have left you in a foul mood. What happened? "

" I haven't had an evening with Tom."

" Didn't you go after all? "

" I went. He didn't come. Sandra came. I've been spending an exhilarating evening with my kid-sister."

I had started towards the kitchen, meaning to make some coffee, but I stopped in the doorway. " What happened? "

Peter went on scowling as he talked. " I went to the pub in Paddington. I arrived a bit early. About ten minutes later Sandra arrived and said she was terribly sorry, Tom had been sent off to the north again. I offered her a drink. She said she'd like one, but not here, she didn't like the place. So we went on to another pub and sat in a corner and talked for about an hour. One or two people spoke to us, obviously taking me for Tom, but Sandra froze them off with a glare. They didn't seem to find that unusual. Her glare seems to be a sort of fixture on her face."

" What did you talk about for a whole hour? " I asked.

" Mostly about her mother and her mother's hard life," Peter said. " I tried to question her about Tom and she said he was all right if you could keep him off the drink, but he was a bit soft and he wouldn't look ahead. He didn't seem to realise this was a world you could get on

in if you gave your mind to it. Then all of a sudden she
seemed to get tired of the pub or my company, said she
wanted to leave now and immediately outside she bolted
into a taxi and went off."

" Did you show her you didn't believe she's your sister?"
I asked.

" No," Peter said.

" I talked the whole thing over with Mr. Barfoot this
evening," I said. " He produced the pleasant suggestion
that they probably want to use you as an alibi for Tom,
while Tom's up to crookery of some sort."

" I'd thought of that too," Peter said unhappily.
" The way to prevent it would be to avoid any more
meetings with any of them in public places. But I still
want to get hold of Tom by himself, Anne."

" Oh, I know," I said. " I'm not trying to stop you."

" For one thing, I want to find out what they're up to."

" Haven't you any suspicion yet what it is? "

" The devil of it is, I've been thinking of everything."

" Well, I find it an awfully uncomfortable feeling, just
sitting waiting for some crime to be committed," I said,
going to the kitchen to fill the kettle and put it on the gas.

Peter's voice followed me. " Always supposing," he
said, " that it hasn't been committed already."

That remark stuck in my mind and next morning on
my way to the office I bought more newspapers than
usual and read them with more than my usual care. I
read every report that I could find of crimes that had
been committed around the time that Peter had spent
with Sandra in the pub in Paddington.

There were, of course, several, from the stealing of
bicycles to sexual assaults. But it wasn't really possible
for me to guess which of these, if any, might have been
Tom's work. I didn't know his line. I didn't know in
which part of the country he operated.

But pondering each crime that might conceivably have

been committed by him, I became more and more depressed. It wasn't only from a fear that if Tom were caught, Peter would soon be involved and might find himself unable to prove that he hadn't known anything about the part that he himself had played. I had the feeling also of something squalid coming close to us, of its following in our footsteps, contaminating the air around us.

Peter met me with the car when I left the office that evening and we drove down to Lachester. It was Dr. Lindsay, that same evening, who unintentionally told us what Tom's activities probably were.

"We're having a lot of excitement around here these days," she said cheerfully, producing sherry in the big sitting-room. "Another burglary. A much bigger haul, I believe, than they got from the Loaders, though perhaps that's only local gossip. It was from Sir Giles Milstrom's house, over at Sandy Green. It hasn't got into the papers yet, because it was only discovered about mid-day. I heard about it from Mrs. Farrier in my afternoon surgery. Her sister's the Milstroms' housekeeper and she spent the evening with the Farriers while the Milstroms were away in London. Apparently she noticed nothing amiss when she went back and it was only when Lady Milstrom opened her jewel-case, or her safe, or whatever it was, to put something back . . ."

Dr. Lindsay stopped, looking from Peter to me.

"What have I said?" she asked. "You both look as if I'd told you that the floor's about to give way under your feet."

Peter stood up quickly and went a walk up and down the length of the room.

"That's just how I feel. In fact, I think it has given way," he said.

"Are you going to explain, or do I have to sit and wonder?" Dr. Lindsay asked.

" I'll explain." He kept up his restless walking up and down the room. Jess, the poodle, who had lost her confidence in me during the interval between my visits, poked a nose out from behind a sofa, as if longing to walk with him, but saw me and retired unhappily into hiding. " Only before I start, Mother, will you promise not to talk about this to anyone else till I agree? "

" I hate giving blindfold promises," she said.

" All right, then I don't think I'll talk," Peter said.

Dr. Lindsay glanced at me, as if considering whether or not I could be induced to talk without making conditions. I smiled and gave a shrug.

" Well, go ahead then—I promise," she said.

Peter came to a standstill with his back to one of the big windows. It was a wet evening and the glass behind him was streaked with little slithering streams of rain.

" Anne told you about seeing a man she mistook for me in the White Horse," Peter said. " Remember? "

" Yes, of course," Dr. Lindsay said.

" We talked about whether or not he was probably my twin brother."

" So you've found him," she said thoughtfully. " Ah well . . . And of course he is."

" Yes, I think he is. I think he's also your burglar."

As her white eyebrows went up, I said, " There's a good deal of guesswork about that, Peter."

" Oh yes," Peter agreed. " In fact, nothing but guesswork. But listen to this." He held out a hand and at each point that he made, checked it off on a finger. " First—Anne meets him, mistakes him for me, tells me about it and so I leave a message for him at the White Horse, asking him to get in touch with me. Second—he does, but not directly. He sends a girl, who says she's his sister—hence my sister too—and Anne and I are invited to their home to meet their mother—my mother—Wait! " Dr. Lindsay had put her hand

suddenly to her head and drawn her breath in sharply.
" Third, this mother of ours turns out to be so young that
she'd have been only about twelve or thirteen when Tom
and I were born, which makes it rather unlikely——"

She interrupted him grimly, " In my profession,
unfortunately, one learns that that's far from unlikely."

" Oh yes." He was tapping his little finger at her,
impatient to get on to his next point. " But Ada Hearn,
as you may remember I found out, was thirty-three
when I born. So this woman wasn't my mother and the
girl wasn't my sister. Fourth—if they want to make me
believe that they are, it's because they think they can
get something out of me, or use me, by playing on my
probable sentiment about my mother. And fifth—"
he stuck his thumb up in the air, and wagged it excitedly
at Dr. Lindsay—" fifth, when I make an arrangement to
meet my brother in a pub, he doesn't turn up, but Sandra
turns up, takes me to another pub where she's sure she's
known, but makes sure no one gets a chance to talk to
me, keeps me there for about an hour, then, just as if
she'd finished a job of work, gets rid of me and goes off.
And when Anne and I talk this over afterwards, it turns
out we've both had the same idea—that I was setting
up an alibi in that pub for Tom, while he was away doing
whatever he does do that needs an alibi! We both thought
of that separately. Well? "

" Yes," Dr. Lindsay said, thrusting a hand through
her white curls. " I see."

Peter started on his fingers again. " Add to that, it
was in this neighbourhood we first encountered Tom,
and when we met on Tuesday evening he went out of his
way, immediately, to explain what he'd been doing here
on Sunday. He and Sandra, he said, had been on their
way to the sea and spent a day on the beach. But it was
that night the Loaders' house was burgled. Second—
Tom and Sandra went back to that pub again later and

I believe they're known there, at least by one man we talked to. And if that's so, that ties them up with this neighbourhood, doesn't it? Third—ever since that business with Sandra last night, I've been looking out for news of something, a burglary, a hold-up, I wasn't sure what, but something that would explain why Sandra kept me talking in that Paddington pub last night. And the first thing you tell us about here is another burglary. Well, when you start being able to predict events correctly, it means you're getting past guesswork, doesn't it? "

"But you've forgotten something, Peter," I said. " If it's that Albert business that makes you say Tom was known in the White Horse, the landlord told us that that man calls everybody Albert."

"Ah yes, and so did Sandra! " Peter cried, turning on me. " That's the point! It's what made me suspicious of her from the start. When she came to the flat to see us, I said I thought my brother's name was Albert and she said, ' Oh, because that drunk in the pub calls him Albert —he calls everyone Albert.' And how could she have known that unless she'd had some experience of Mr. Biggs? "

"Biggs? " Dr. Lindsay said. " George Biggs? "

"Yes," Peter said. " Do you know him? "

"I know a George Biggs who's recently taken over an old junk-shop at Sandy Green," she said. " A terrible old liar. And an alcoholic who oughtn't to be allowed on the roads. I had to patch up a schoolgirl who'd had to send her bicycle into the ditch to get out of the way of his van."

"Isn't Sandy Green the place where the burglary happened last night? " I said.

Dr. Lindsay said that it was and also that it was the old village, near to the White Horse, which had been engulfed by the suburbs of Lachester. We all looked at one another then as if we had arrived somewhere.

She went on, " I'm beginning to regret giving you that promise, Peter. If I hadn't, I think I'd ring up Inspector Belden straight away and tell him everything you've told me." She stood up and went towards the door.

In swift anxiety, he asked, " Where are you going? "

" Only to dish up. Don't worry—I won't go near the telephone. But perhaps when you've thought things over, you'll ring Belden up yourself."

" There's something else I want to do first," Peter answered.

" Oh, I know—you want to find Tom," she said. " You want to save him from himself—for *yourself*—isn't that it? But I think myself you're a little late in the day. Tom's part of a world, just as you are yourself, and d'you think his will let him go, even if he ever wants it to? It's a world that doesn't let go, you know, of body or soul."

She went out.

Peter turned to the window and stood staring out into the bleak, gusty twilight. There was something despondent but very stubborn about his slight figure, outlined against the streaming sky.

After a short silence, he said, " I'm going to the White Horse this evening, Anne. There's no need for you to come unless you want to."

" Oh, I'll come," I said, " though what good it'll do . . ."

" I want to talk to George Biggs."

" Dr. Lindsay isn't going to like it."

" We needn't stay long," he said, as if it were only our absence on our first evening with her that his mother wasn't going to like.

In fact, when he told her at dinner what we were going to do afterwards, she seemed already to have assumed that that was what we would do. Over dinner we talked about the foolishness of keeping valuable jewels at home, where they were nothing but a temptation to thieves, and we all sounded pleased with ourselves for avoiding foolishness of that kind so successfully. We even agreed that it was foolishness to possess valuable jewels at all, when semi-precious stones were generally so much more attractive. I don't think we went so far as to say that we would refuse a present of diamonds, if it were offered, but there were many things, we thought, which we should far prefer, which wouldn't make it essential for us to have burglar alarms on our windows.

Immediately after dinner, promising not to be gone long, Peter and I set off for the White Horse.

We were nearly there when Peter exclaimed, " I'm a fool! There's an old red pullover and some flannels in my room at home. I ought to have changed."

" You mean you're going in there pretending to be Tom! "

I found I disliked that idea extremely.

" I don't mean to go as far as that," Peter said. " I thought I'd just stroll in and if old Biggs is there, see if he seemed to know me or not. Then, when he'd given himself away, I'd be very innocently surprised at his having been able to mistake me."

" That won't make him tell you anything about Tom," I said.

" No, but it may tell me a little about Biggs."

" If that's what you want, I'd better hang back a bit when you go to the pub," I said. " If he sees me with you, he'll know at once which one you are."

" All right, you can stay in the car for a minute or two after I go in," Peter said, as we turned into the car-park, sending up a spray from the puddles in the asphalt and stopping between a Jaguar and Geo. Biggs's van, which was in its accustomed place.

There were not many other cars there, the wet evening having kept a good deal of custom away. As Peter got out I lit a cigarette and went on puffing at it conscientiously for about three minutes. Then I got out too and followed him inside.

I saw Mr. Biggs immediately. He was in his usual corner, in his loose brown overall and his felt hat and he had his elbows on the bar and his face held between his fists. He was staring straight before him, talking to nobody.

For a moment I did not see Peter. There were three or four men standing in a group near the bar, but Peter wasn't one of them. I looked round and there he was, penned in a corner, sitting at one of the little round tables and held there as immovably as if he had been lashed to his chair by the hands of Margaret Loader, clasping his arm.

CHAPTER VII

THE BIG DIAMOND flashed on Margaret's hand. She was wearing her necklace of small pearls with a dress of light blue jersey and a dark blue three-quarter length coat. She was talking rapidly into Peter's ear and though his head was half-turned away from her and he was staring down at his hands, I saw at once the tension in his body. Neither of them had seen me.

I had time, standing there, to think that Peter turned into another person when he was with Margaret. He turned into a person trying to strangle all the normal warmth of feeling in him and who went pale and ugly with the effort. He all but trembled at her touch. And Margaret's eyes dwelt on him with an intensity tinged with unhappy understanding, which left no doubt in my mind that she was as much in love with him as she had ever been, or even more, perhaps, because she had lost him. And I had no doubt that Peter knew it.

I didn't know where Owen came in and I thought that Margaret herself might not quite know it either. Perhaps she had never imagined that marriage to him would mean that she must wholly give up Peter, that Peter himself would see it so. Even now she did not seem able to believe that he could really mean to tear himself away from her.

It was Owen, returning from the bar with drinks for them all, who saw me first. He said my name in surprise and Peter heard it and started up.

Margaret did not quite let go of him. Letting one hand slide down to his wrist, she encircled it tightly with her fingers. But she beckoned me to a chair beside her, giving me a brief, sweet smile, then turned again to Peter, to ask him why he hadn't mentioned the fact that I was there too.

" Didn't I? " he said vaguely.

Owen asked me what I would like to drink and returned to the bar to fetch it.

" I've just been telling Peter all about our burglary," Margaret said. " I was frantic—truly frantic to begin with. I couldn't believe it. I just stood there looking at the open safe and feeling absolutely convinced that I was seeing things. Well, not actually convinced, but you know what I mean. I couldn't, I wouldn't take in what it meant. It felt so horrible! And so unbelievable! I mean, why should any burglar pick on *my* jewellery? How did he know about it? How did he know when we'd be out? And then the police were maddening, because instead of trying to cheer me up about it, they read me a lecture on keeping things like that at home, and leaving bathroom windows open and made me feel they probably suspected me of having arranged it all myself to collect the insurance. I've decided I hate the police. I've always thought they looked so wonderful and reliable and efficient, driving about in their fast cars. But as soon

as you want them for anything, it turns out they can't
leave the telephone in the police station and they take
hours—literally hours—to arrive. And then they sneer
at you for having your jewellery stolen."

She was half laughing and half protesting in earnest.

Owen, bringing my drink and sitting down, said with
a curtness that I hadn't heard in his voice before, " We've
been over all this rather often, haven't we? "

" Have we? " she said. " Oh, but I haven't had a
chance to tell Peter all about it properly."

Peter raised his eyes to Margaret's, " Do you often
come here? " he asked.

" Oh no, darling," she said, " not often. Just occasionally, because Owen doesn't seem to care for our local
for some reason." Her voice and her look told me that
their local was associated in Owen's mind with meetings
between her and Peter. " Seeing you come in was a
lovely surprise."

" Do you know that man in the corner? " Peter
asked.

Owen answered, " George Biggs? He's got a shop of
sorts in Sandy Green. I've never been into it, because
it's hardly ever open. It's just a dump, where he seems
to sell everything from brass bedsteads and old stoves to
curling tongs. I always marvel how that kind of place
keeps going, because you never see anyone buying
anything there, but he must do all right, because the
amount he spends in here on double whiskies would
keep a family in luxury."

" He's rather a poppet," Margaret said, " with an
unlimited supply of incredible stories. But if you ever see
his van on the road, keep well out of the way. If he
never gets really drunk, he's never quite sober."

" I wouldn't describe him as a poppet," Owen said.
" I'd call him a quarrelsome and conceited old liar.
Arthur Galpin—he's the landlord—used to try to stop

him coming here. He said the way Biggs buttonholed people and bored them with his yarns did more damage to the place than all the money he spent here was worth."

He stopped as George Biggs suddenly swung round. "Albert!" he shouted.

But it was not at Peter that he was staring with his small, furtive, alcoholic's eyes. It was at the door, where a man in a motor-cyclist's helmet, goggles and leggings, was standing stripping off a streaming windjacket before coming farther in.

"Look at Albert the Spacerider!" cried Mr. Biggs. "What's it like on the moon, Albert?"

"Bloody cold and no beer," the cyclist answered, and taking off his helmet showed the face of Tom Hearn.

As he did so, he saw the group of us in the corner.

His face went white and his eyes blazed with panic. Margaret gave an incredulous gasp. Her hands went to her mouth as if to shut in a cry. Peter jumped to his feet. But before he could dodge round the table, Tom had turned on his heel and vanished and by the time that Peter had reached the door, a motor-cycle was roaring away up the road.

Peter returned after a moment. His jacket was rain-spotted and his hair windblown. He told the Loaders abruptly that we had to go now and in spite of their protests, started to hustle me out. But as he was doing so, Mr. Galpin came over to us, leaving his wife in charge of the bar.

"That damn' man," Mr. Galpin muttered to us confidentially with a sidelong glance at Mr. Biggs. "I've done all I can to get him to take his custom elsewhere, short of watering his drinks. That'd shift him, I should think, but it isn't legal. He's a public nuisance. No wonder that young chap bolted out. I'm sorry about that. You came in here looking for him, I imagine."

The eyes in his purplish face were keen and inquisitive.
I wondered if he could really believe that Tom had bolted
because of Mr. Biggs's shouted greeting.

" I didn't, as a matter of fact," Peter said. " I've
met him since I was here last and I thought he was away
in the north—which reminds me, I haven't thanked you
for giving him our address."

" Oh, that's all right," Mr. Galpin said. " He and
the girl came back later that same evening. If you'll
forgive my asking—are you related? "

" Well, yes, in a way," Peter said, nudging me again
towards the door.

Mr. Galpin took the hint.

" Well, good night, sir. Good night, madam. Hope
to see you back. But really it's such an extraordinary
resemblance. . . ."

He returned to the bar. Peter and I went out into the
rain and got into the car.

I discovered that Peter was in an extremely bad
temper.

" Why should the mere sight of me make Tom turn
and bolt for his life like that? " he demanded bitterly
as we swung into the roundabout. " What have I done
to him? What does he think I want to do to him? "

" Perhaps it wasn't just seeing you," I said.

" But that's all that happened. I didn't speak to him.
I never had a chance to speak to him."

" He saw you with the Loaders, though. He didn't see
just you, he saw you with two of his victims," I said.

Peter calmed down a little.

" I didn't think of that. . . . Oh well, there's nothing
to be done about it now. He'll have to make the next
move."

" What happened about Mr. Biggs when you went in? "
I asked. " Didn't he see you? "

" He saw me, but so did Margaret and she called out

my name, so whether because he knew I wasn't Tom, or just because he wasn't feeling sociable, he turned his back and went into a quiet huddle with himself."

"We could try visiting him in his shop to-morrow morning," I suggested.

"I don't think we'd get anything out of him. He'd be on the lookout and be very careful. Oh, let's forget the whole damned thing!"

That seemed to me a wonderful idea, only I didn't think for a moment that Peter meant it.

Yet perhaps, if it had been possible, he would have done his best to forget Tom Hearn after that evening. The way that Tom had turned and fled at sight of him seemed to go on rankling. That meant, I supposed, that Peter had been building even more than I had realised on the thought of his twin brother, and the discovery that his own existence meant nothing to that brother except perhaps some form of menace, was a shock that hurt. At all events next day Peter said nothing about Tom or Sandra or Ivy May until, about half-way through the morning, the telephone rang and Mrs. Joy, who answered it, came to tell him that a lady wanted to speak to him.

Peter was gone from the room for about five minutes. When he returned he said, "That was Mum. My dear Mum, Anne."

"Ivy May?" I said.

"Yes, but still calling herself Ada Hearn, and saying she wants to see us. She's all in a stew, she says, because of something Tom's done."

"When does she want to see us?"

"This afternoon at about three."

"But we can't go back to London to-day," I said. "Dr. Lindsay thinks we're staying for the whole week-end."

"Mum didn't say anything about London. She

suggested a café called the Kettle on the Hob somewhere on the London road, about five miles the other side of Lachester. I've written down her directions."

He gave me a smile as he said this, standing there in front of me with a watchful glance on my face, to see how I was going to take it. Then he stooped over me and gave me a light kiss on the forehead.

At his touch I felt a hot surge of anger inside me. It took me by surprise, it came so swiftly and fiercely, so that for a moment I could not answer. Yet it was not a new anger. It was something with which I had been living for the last week. It came from a sense of having been cheated, given delusions for a little while of my own shining and glorious worth to another human being, only to find that apparently I was really of far less account, less interest, than a despicable gang of crooks.

It was a relief to feel this anger. It drove out the scared feeling that had haunted me all this time. I gripped the arms of my chair and sat up straighter.

" Peter, there's something I think I should tell you," I said and was pleased with the cold decision in my voice. " I'm getting very, very tired of those people. And I think it's time you got a little bit realistic with yourself about the kind of people they are."

" Oh God! " Peter said impatiently, " Listen, Anne, it's like this——"

" I know just what it's like," I said, hearing how my voice had begun to shake with my anger. " You'll go to meet that woman because you think she'll tell you something about Tom. But she won't. Perhaps she won't even be there. Perhaps it'll be Sandra again. And while you and Sandra are together, perhaps there'll be another burglary somewhere. And what will you do then—go to the police or wait till they come for you ? And whichever you do, how are you going to convince them you didn't know anything about what Tom was up to? Because you do know now. You know really quite a lot about it. And they'll get that out of you. And on top of all this, you think—you think you've only got to give me that disarming smile and I'll let you go on and on till you're in serious trouble. You expect me to sit here and—and——"

" Anne, please! " Peter said. " If you'll just listen a moment . . ."

But it seemed to me that there was no sign on his face that he had been listening to me. There was no sign either that he had the slightest intention of changing his mind about going to meet Ivy May.

" You quiet people! " I said, bringing a fist crashing down on the arm of my chair, " Margaret was right— you nice, quiet people always say you'll do just what one wants and then—and then you don't even bother to find out *what* one wants——"

I might have said a lot more, but at that point Peter, whose face had gone white, turned and went quietly out of the room.

The echoes of my own voice seemed to take a long time to die in it. Then the front door slammed and I heard swift footsteps walking away from the house.

I sat where I was for some minutes, gradually relaxing in the chair. Jess, who had followed Peter out of the room, but had been shut into the house when he left it, came back and unexpectedly laid her head on my knee. I pulled one of her ears and she gave a half-hearted wag of her tail.

I sat where I was for some time, waiting to hear the footsteps coming back. My anger hadn't really left me, and the fact that Peter hadn't blazed back at me, had said so little and then simply gone away, was fuel on the flames. But I was beginning to dislike the feeling of that harsh, useless heat.

Gazing idly at the window, through which I saw grey,

clumsy masses of cloud moving across the sky and some
poplars straining and shivering in the gusty wind, I
wondered what would happen next. What did Peter do
if one insisted on quarrelling with him? I didn't know.
And it was a strange thought that I was married to a man
about whom I didn't know a thing like that. Strange and
rather absurd. A belief that there had been something
rather absurd about everything that had happened in the
last few weeks began to seep into my mind and cooled
my anger into chill desperation.

Hadn't there been fantastic absurdity, humiliating
absurdity in the eagerness with which I had grasped at
love without having even begun to understand the man
who had offered it to me; without, for instance, having
the insight to know in my bones whether at the moment,
he was walking up and down the garden, only a few
yards away from me, chewing his nails in a frenzy of
unpromising plots of how to deal with me, or was miles
away already, driving to London and not meaning to
turn back?

It would have been easy, of course, to go into the
garden and see. But I didn't seem to have the will to do
anything but listen for returning footsteps. The only
ones that I presently heard, however, were the heavy,
deliberate footsteps of Dr. Lindsay, returning home for
lunch after a round of calls in Lachester.

When she saw me sitting there alone, she asked me
where Peter was and I told her that he had been rung up
by Mrs. May and had gone to meet her. I said it as
casually as I could, but she gave me one of those glances
of hers which lingered uncomfortably long on my face
and were so full of a weary sort of understanding that
although she said nothing about it, I was sure that she
had recognised in me the traces of my quarrel with Peter.

At lunch I thought that she was irritable, as if I had
failed her in something. But I doubted if she could have

stopped Peter going to meet Mrs. May any more than I could. We ate our boiled silverside and dumplings and our baked apples and custard almost in silence, until, just after the meal, the telephone rang again.

The call was again for Peter. Mrs. Joy put her head in at the door to tell us so, then returned to the telephone to say that he was not available. A moment later she returned.

" He says if Mr. Peter's not here, can he speak to Mrs. Peter, please? " she said.

I went out, picked the telephone up and said, " Hallo."

" Anne? " said the voice of Tom Hearn. He sounded breathless and in a hurry, and didn't trouble to tell me who was speaking. " Look, it's important—can't I speak to Pete? "

" He's out, Tom," I said.

" But I've got to get hold of him, Anne! When'll he be back? "

" I'm not sure." I could have told him that Peter was probably on his way to meet Ivy May, but if Tom didn't know that, if the gang was not working as one, perhaps it would be as well not to inform him. " Sometime this afternoon, I think. Lateish, probably."

There was a pause.

Then he went on, " No good. I've got to go up north again to-night and I wanted to tell him before I left . . . But if I can't, I can't."

I thought he was going to ring off, so I said quickly, " Where are you, Tom? "

" In Lachester."

" Where in Lachester? "

" In the post office. Why? "

" I wondered if it would be any use if I came instead of Peter."

" Well—maybe," he said doubtfully. " Yes—I dare say it would. Can you manage it? "

" Yes—or you could come here," I suggested.

" No," he said at once. " I'm not getting mixed up in anything like that, thank you. Pete's people are nothing to do with me. You come along here if you want to and I'll tell you about that business in the pub last night. Why I cleared out. I want Pete to know about it—for his own good, see—in case I don't see him again. But I'm not getting mixed up with his lot."

" Why d'you think you may not see him again? " I asked. " Aren't you coming back from the north? "

" I'll tell you about that when I see you," he said. " Well, maybe I will. Not that it makes any odds. But it'll be better for Pete if I drop out. You tell him I said so. Look—will you do that, Anne? "

" Where shall I meet you? "

" Here outside the post office'll do. Make it about three o'clock. But listen—will you tell him to keep clear of us, Anne? You've got a head on your shoulders. You know it's best for him. But tell him I said so—me, Tom."

There was a click and the dialling tone began.

I put the telephone down, went back to the sitting-room and told Dr. Lindsay what had happened.

She sat frowning, stirring her coffee.

" If only he hadn't said three o'clock, I think I'd have come with you and got a glimpse of this mysterious character," she said. " But I've a surgery from two to three-thirty. Is it any use my advising you not to get on to his motor-bike with him, or go anywhere that isn't thoroughly in the public eye? "

" Outside the post office sounds fairly public," I said, " How do I get there? "

" There's a bus at two-fifty from just a little way up the road here," she said. " I'd drive you in, but you'd have rather a long time to hang about in Lachester. And the bus takes you to almost opposite the post office."

She told me where to find the bus stop, said she hoped I really would use my common sense and not do anything stupid, and left me again.

I read a newspaper for a little while, seeing a report of the burglary at Sandy Green in which it was stated that the value of the jewels stolen from Lady Milstrom was estimated at twenty-five thousand pounds. Thinking that that put the Loaders' burglary almost into the same class as the theft of a few pairs of nylon stockings or a bottle of whisky, I put on a coat and, at a quarter to three, started out to the bus stop.

Jess was in the garden and took it into her whimsical head that she now trusted me enough to go for a walk with me. This was a nuisance and I had to put on a show of anger to persuade her to stay behind. Disillusioned, she crept away into a clump of rhododendrons. It was starting to rain again as I went. The rain was not very heavy, but there was enough wind to drive it stingingly into my face. The bus stop was about a hundred yards up a slight hill, beyond the house, coming from Lachester, and although the road had hedges on each side, they did not give much shelter. Turning my coat-collar up, I fished in my hand-bag for my plastic hood, tied it over my hair, and walked along with my head bent, dodging the puddles left behind by last night's steady rain.

I wasn't watching the traffic that went by, so I was taken by surprise when a car stopped beside me, just before I reached the bus stop and I heard my name called.

The car was the Loaders' Jaguar and it was Owen who had called me. He was alone.

" I'm going into Lachester—can I take you anywhere?" he asked.

Gratefully, I slithered in beside him and the car moved on, past Dr. Lindsay's house and towards the town.

" Tell me where you'd like to be dropped," Owen

said. " I'm going right into town—I can make it any-where."

" If it isn't out of your way then, can you take me to the post office? " I said.

" The post office! " The big car slid to a stop. " I knew I'd forgotten something. Look, d'you mind frightfully if we go back for it? It'll only take me a minute or two. My publisher's been badgering me for my proofs for a month and I swore faithfully I'd get them off this week-end."

I looked doubtfully at my watch. " I've an appoint-ment at three—a rather important appointment. Perhaps I'd better take the bus after all."

" Three? We can manage that easily," Owen said, starting to back the car into a driveway and turn it. " The parcel's all ready on my table. I've only to pop in and pick it up."

We swung across the road and started back the way we had come.

As we did so, the bus came into view and I knew that I had missed it, so there was nothing to be done but stay where I was and hope that Owen meant what he had said. He was, at any rate, a fast driver, and we were outside Long Grange in a few minutes.

It was a small Queen Anne house, very attractive, with only a strip of lawn and a row of low white posts, with chains strung from one to the next, between it and the road. Owen told me to stay where I was and hurried into the house. In a moment he was back again with a parcel which he threw into the back of the car.

" You've plenty of time—don't look so worried," he said as he got in again beside me. " And if it's Peter you're meeting, why not just let him wait? "

" As a matter of fact, it isn't Peter," I said.

" I promise to get you there on time, anyway." He turned the car and started back towards Lachester. " I'm glad, as it happens, to have this chance to talk to you."

We were passing a lay-by on the left as he said this. It had been empty as we went up the hill to his house, but in the few minutes since then, a small van had pulled up in it. It was Geo. Biggs's van, and Geo. Biggs himself was slumped over the wheel, asleep. I remember I almost commented on this to Owen, but he was going on talking, so I did not interrupt him.

"I'm going to be awfully personal," he said, "and hope you'll forgive me, because what I want to do is relieve your mind of some quite needless distress. Go on and tell me, if you want to, that the distress doesn't exist, but I was watching your face yesterday evening and I think it does. And truly, it's quite needless."

"Yesterday——?"

"In the White Horse. As I said, I was watching you——"

I did interrupt him then with an exclamation. For as we shot past Dr. Lindsay's house, I saw Peter in the garden. He was standing on the lawn with Jess gambolling around him, welcoming him home with her usual ecstatic affection.

I almost asked Owen to stop the car again, so that we could pick Peter up, but Owen had gone on with what he had been saying and because of what it was I let him drive straight on.

"—I was watching you and I could see what it does to you to watch Margaret with Peter," he said. "I've been through it myself—otherwise I don't suppose I'd have the nerve to talk about it like this. But I'd like to cheer you up, and convince you that it doesn't mean anything. It's just a sort of—well, an old habit of hers, a childish habit."

"How long have you been married?" I asked him rather grimly.

"About six months—but it was the same from the start

and will probably be the same in ten years' time. I suppose I'd like it to stop—I'm quite normally jealous—but I'm not going to break my heart if it doesn't. As I said, it doesn't mean anything."

The repetition of the phrase somehow carried less conviction than it had the first time.

" I don't believe I could stand ten years of it," I said. " I should take drastic action of some kind."

" My dear Anne, I take drastic action about once a week," he said. " Margaret thrives on it. Truly, the only thing is not to take the thing seriously. They aren't in love."

" But they have been."

" Oh yes. But don't tell me you've never been in love with anyone but Peter."

" But in my own case I know that it's over, don't I?" I said.

He gave me a quick glance. " I don't seem to have made much impression. I mean in the way of providing reassurance. Because that's what I was trying to do, having had to work all this out for myself in the past. I like you, Anne, and I don't like to see you worrying yourself about it. After all, Peter doesn't play up to her, does he? "

" I'm not sure I'd mind it as much if he did," I said. " If he could just take seeing her cheerfully, Owen, not resist so hard, not go so tense, not *suffer* quite so much, I believe I'd care far less. But he went through something pretty bad with Margaret, and whatever you say, it doesn't seem to be really over yet."

We had just turned into the main street of Lachester, the street with the fine old half-timbered houses with the chain-store shop-fronts. It was narrow and there was a good deal of traffic. Owen had to concentrate on his driving.

" They've known each other for years, you know," he

said in a more absent tone, looking for a parking-space
beside the crowded pavement. " You and I are relatively
strangers to them. And that probably gives us some
advantage. It's easy to know a person too well."

" It's awfully difficult to know them well enough,"
I said.

" But there's no hurry. You've a lifetime to put in on
the job." He found an empty space and steered the
Jaguar into it, twisted in his seat and reached into the
back of the car for the parcel of proofs that he had tossed
there. " There's more than enough rush in life, don't
you think? " He gave me his warm smile as he got out
of the car.

I smiled back and was getting out too when a very
upsetting thought occurred to me. It was that as Owen
had a parcel to post, we should approach the post office
together.

I could have told him, I suppose, whom I was going to
meet and asked him to let me go ahead alone because I
was afraid Tom might turn and flee, as he had the night
before, if he saw me arriving with one of the Loaders.
Yet if Tom was waiting, I had probably been observed
already, getting out of the Jaguar. For the post office
was only twenty yards or so down the street. So I said
nothing to Owen about letting me go ahead and we walked
the short distance side by side, then Owen went into the
post office and I stood, sheltering from the rain, in the
entrance.

After a few minutes Owen came out again. He made
a little gesture of farewell as he passed me and strode off to
the car. I went on waiting. For about ten minutes I
didn't worry much, then I began to say to myself that
after all I had arrived late and so Tom hadn't waited for me.
Or perhaps, although I hadn't seen him, he had seen me
with Owen and had been frightened off. Or perhaps
something else had happened to him. Or perhaps, since

he couldn't see Peter, he had never really intended to come. There had been something in the last few things that he had said to me which had sounded as if perhaps he hadn't.

I went over all the possibilities a number of times, waiting on the steps of the post office for twenty-five minutes. Then, seeing the bus coming that would take me back to where I had come from, I gave up and ran for it.

It was only when I got off the bus presently and started the short walk back to the house that I began to wonder what I should do if Peter hadn't stayed at home. For Dr. Lindsay would not have returned home yet and I hadn't been given a latch-key.

Ringing the front-door bell produced frantic barking from Jess inside the house, but no sound of footsteps approaching the door. Waiting in the chilling rain, I rang twice more. Jess's startled barking changed to a rather horrible howling, but that was all. I felt no doubt that she was by herself in the house and was lonely and frightened.

Thinking that perhaps I might find some ground-floor window open, I started off round the house. I was not particularly hopeful. The day had turned so completely into the kind of day on which nothing goes right that it felt only natural now to find myself shut out in the rain. The sound of Jess's wailing followed me from window to window, all of which were securely fastened.

Then I heard another sound. It was that of a door banging in the wind. I went on and found that it was the back door, which was not only unlocked but standing open.

As I reached it, it closed in my face, but it had not latched itself and at once swung open again. Going in, I closed it behind me and began to peel off my wet mackintosh. The noise I made coming in had silenced

Jess for a moment, but now she started again, and on a new note of frenzy and I heard her hurl herself, with scrabbling claws, at the other side of the closed door that led from the kitchen to the hall.

Something in that howling suddenly gave me cold shivers.

" Shut up, Jess! " I shouted at her.

She leapt at the door again. I dropped my mackintosh on the floor, crossed the kitchen and pulled the door open.

Jess shrank back before me. The howling changed to a desperate little whine. Crouching, she sidled away from me to the foot of the stairs, trying to lead me towards the dead man who was lying at the bottom of them.

CHAPTER VIII

THERE IS a complete blankness for me over the next moments, because of course I thought the man was Peter. He had Peter's narrow face and aquiline nose, and curly fair hair. The staring brown eyes in the dead, drained face were Peter's. He was wearing what looked just like Peter's grey suit and he was in Peter's home. The only thing about him which it seemed impossible should be a part of Peter was the mess of blood all over his white shirt and the hands that clutched at it.

Then Peter's voice spoke behind me, his arms clasped me and I began to come out of the blankness with the memory that there were two Peters. It was the other, it was Tom Hearn, who was dead. Wasn't it? . . .

I turned to Peter, putting my arms round his neck, clinging to him, needing to feel the whole familiarity of his body.

" Yes, it's me—it's *me*, Anne! " he said, almost as if he

doubted it himself. " Come along—come out of here."

" But we ought to do something. . . ." I said helplessly, trying to resist as he started to lead me out to the kitchen.

" There's nothing we can do for him," Peter said. He pushed me into a chair, went back to the door and closed it. Then he went to the back door and closed that too and locked it.

I was still stupid with shock, and asked vaguely, " Why did you do that? "

" So that no one can get in," he said.

" Who would try? "

" I don't know. I must have been thinking of the murderer. It doesn't matter." His voice was jerky. " Wait here a moment."

He went back to the other door and through it to the hall, closing it again behind him.

I tried to get up then, thinking that I must open that locked door and go out into the garden and breathe, because there seemed to be no air in the kitchen. But my feet felt too far away to do what was expected of them. I was trying to send them instructions, which they still wouldn't understand, when Peter returned, bringing Jess with him.

He gave me a look, went to the sink, filled a glass with cold water and brought it to me. Drinking it, I looked hazily at Jess, knowing that there was something I wanted to say about her. But the blankness was still there in my mind, leaving queer, empty spaces in my memory.

Peter stood close to me, looking down at me. As I handed back the glass, he said, " I think he was shot, Anne. Through the heart. I haven't touched him, and I don't know much about these things. I haven't seen anybody who's been shot before. . . . Well, I'm sure he was shot. But the fantastic thing is, he seems to have been after Mother's jewellery."

I thought there was something fantastic about Peter's

finding fantastic just that particular fact in the whole fantastic situation.

" Have you called the police? " I asked.

" No, I'll do that in a minute." He sat down on the edge of the kitchen table. " Tell me what happened."

I had just been going to ask him that, but since he had got the question in first, I answered, " I just came in—I came in this way, because the front door was locked—and I found him. That's all. I'd just found him when you came back and found me."

" When did you go out? " Peter asked.

" Just before you came back," I said.

" No, Anne. Please try to think. Tom's been dead for—well, for more than a few minutes. That much I can tell."

" But that's what I said—I went to catch the bus," I said, " then actually I was given a lift into Lachester by Owen Loader."

" You've been into Lachester? "

" Yes."

" But then you must have gone out ages ago and you just said you went out only just before I got back."

" Yes. About a quarter to three," I said.

" I wasn't here then," he said.

" But I saw you in the garden just afterwards—about five to three, I think."

He gave his head a shake, as if he were trying to clear a singing in the ears.

" About five to three I was the other side of Lachester, looking for that damned Kettle on the Hob, which doesn't exist. If you think you saw me . . ."

He paused. Both our heads turned, as if a voice had called us, towards the door behind which Tom Hearn lay dead. Then we looked back at one another. At the same moment, knowing what Peter was going to say next, I remembered what I had wanted to say about Jess.

He said what I was expecting. And it was a lie.

"You saw Tom, Anne."

I knew it was a lie because of Jess. For although if Peter had been alone in the garden, I couldn't possibly have said which of the brothers I had seen, of one thing I was certain and that was that to Jess there would have been no difficulty in distinguishing between her dearly loved and trusted Peter and the terrifying stranger, Tom. And it hadn't been a stranger around whom I had seen her happily gambolling at a quarter to three.

Peter and I seemed to go on looking at one another for a long time. While we did so, it crossed my mind that there is no one who looks one so steadily and calmly in the eye as someone who is telling a considered lie. But this lie of Peter's had cleared the fuzziness out of my brain, bringing me to myself as sharply as a slap in the face.

"It was you I saw, Peter," I said, "and for heaven's sake don't pretend it wasn't—I mean to me, or the police either, because I may not have been the only person who saw you."

"Anne, will you listen to me?" he said softly. "You did *not* see me. If you saw anyone, it was Tom. At five to three I was still hunting up and down the London road for a café called the Kettle on the Hob, which no one I asked had ever heard of. I don't think it exists. I think Ivy May rang me up and asked me to meet her there simply to get me out of the house. Now tell me how they got you out of the house."

"Peter, I know it was you I saw," I said. "Please trust me! We've got to call the police in a moment——"

"For God's sake!" he broke in, hitting the kitchen table with the flat of his hand. "You saw Tom. If you doubt me, ask Margaret. I picked her up at the bus stop near the White Horse at about a quarter to three and when I gave up trying to find the Kettle on the Hob I gave her a lift home before I came here. Now tell me, how did they get you out of the house? "

" Margaret! "

If he hadn't spoken that name, I should have told him about Jess and given him a chance to try to explain her away, but suddenly the fact that Margaret was involved in his lying to me made it feel impossible to go on trying to persuade him to trust me. Let him put his trust in Margaret!

I gave a shrug of my shoulders. " Tom rang up," I said. " He wanted you. I didn't tell him you'd gone to meet Ivy May, but I said you wouldn't be back till the late afternoon. He said he couldn't wait. But it was important, he said. He said he wanted to see you to explain something about the way he bolted when he saw you last night. I asked if it would be any use if I came instead, and we made an appointment to meet outside the post office at three. Only he never turned up."

" Of course he didn't, they just wanted the two of us out of the house," Peter said. " They knew Mother would be at her afternoon surgery and Mrs. Joy would have gone home. With you and me out of the way, Tom had a clear field for his operations."

" But it was you Tom wanted, because he was going away and thought he might not see you again," I said. " And he told me to tell you that it would be best for you if he dropped out and he wanted me particularly to say it was he who said so. He can't have known anything about Ivy May ringing you up first."

" But he spoke to you, didn't he? " Peter said. " And he saw that you went to meet him."

" You mean it was really me he wanted all the time? "

" He was probably checking up to make sure we'd both gone off to meet Ivy May. And finding that you hadn't, he managed things so that you'd go to meet him. But there's one thing I simply can't understand, Anne ... "

Peter stared down at the floor, as if he were trying to read the answer to his problem in the worn pattern of the linoleum. " Tom seems to have come here to steal Mother's jewellery. Mother's jewellery! If the whole lot's worth fifty pounds, it'd surprise me. And we've been thinking of Tom as someone who went after loot worth thousands—and who had fairly precise information about it too. So coming here after Mother's garnets and seed-pearls seems complete lunacy."

" How do you know he came here to steal? " I asked.

" One of her seed-pearl ear-rings is on the floor beside him," Peter said. " And I took a quick look in her room. She's got an old ivory box she kept the things in and it's open and empty."

As he spoke of the seed-pearls, I had a very foolish thought. Pearls again. White beads. For twins, portents of evil. . . .

" Where are they all now? " I asked, and was going on to ask him if he thought that Tom had been murdered for the sake of those jewels, which had been hardly worth stealing in the first place, when we both heard the grating sound of a key being thrust into the lock of the front door. Peter sprang to the kitchen door and was in the hall to meet Dr. Lindsay, standing between her and the body at the foot of the stairs, as she came in.

He had had some idea of preparing her for what she would see, but as her gaze went past him she brushed him aside with brusque authority and strode forward. I saw her stoop quickly over Tom, peering into his face, then glance up at Peter, seeing the likeness, hardly believing in it, but knowing that she had no time to think of it now.

" You've called the police, of course," she said, as she straightened up again.

" No, as a matter of fact——"

" You haven't? Are you mad? "

She strode to the alcove where the telephone was and snatched it up. Dialling hastily, she went on, " How long ago did it happen? "

" I don't know," Peter said. " We were both out——"

She interrupted him to speak into the telephone to someone at the police station, asking him if she could speak to Inspector Belden.

In a moment she had been put through to Inspector Belden and was telling him that there had been murder in her house. I realised from the way she spoke that he was someone whom she knew well, either an old friend or an old enemy, I couldn't have said for certain which, since the sizzling indignation in her tone just then seemed to include everyone and everything. But her briefness and directness showed that she felt she could take his understanding for granted.

Ringing off, she turned on Peter, concentrating her indignation on him.

" Come along," she said, marching towards the sitting-room. " I want to be told what happened—and quickly, because we haven't got long. You too, Anne. I want to know what the two of you thought you were doing here, apparently waiting for the police to arrive on the scene by instinct. Couldn't you see you'd got a murder on your hands? Didn't you know it was your duty to call the police immediately? "

Following her, Peter answered coolly, " We knew all those things and quite a number more, but you sound much too agitated to be told any of them, so why don't we simply have a drink and give ourselves a chance to calm down? I should like to be very calm and collected when we meet Inspector Belden."

He was very calm and collected already, far more so than when he had been talking with me. A long-established habit of defence against Dr. Lindsay's force-fulness wiped all the expression out of his face. It was

D

unlikely, I thought, that Dr. Lindsay would find out anything useful from him.

She had tossed her handbag and gloves on to a chair and had gone to stand on the hearthrug, a small, powerful figure with an angry, tired face.

" We haven't time for a drink," she said. " When did you find—your brother? "

" A few minutes ago," Peter answered.

" Were you and Anne together? "

" All but."

" What do you mean—all but? Were you or weren't you? "

He sat down on the arm of a chair and swung one foot.

" I think we'd get along better if you let me tell it in my own way," he said. " Then let Anne tell her bit in her way."

" Very well," she said. " Go ahead."

" It began this morning when I was rung up by Mum—that's to say, the woman who calls herself Ada Hearn. She said she wanted to see Anne and me at a place called the Kettle on the Hob, about five miles the other side of Lachester along the London road, because she'd got to talk to me about something Tom had done. We arranged to meet there at three o'clock."

" But you left here long before that," Dr. Lindsay said, " and Anne didn't go with you."

" I know—Anne and I had a row and I went into Lachester and had lunch by myself. Then I went on to look for the Kettle on the Hob. On the way I picked up Margaret at the bus stop near the White Horse—that was at about a quarter to three—and she came with me, looking for this café that didn't exist, then I took her home to Long Grange, then I came back here."

" What was Margaret doing at a bus stop? " Dr. Lindsay asked.

" Waiting for a bus," Peter said.

" I didn't know Margaret used the buses."

Peter's face went a little paler. " She was at the bus stop. And she said something about Owen having the car, and Anne will corroborate that, because he gave her a lift in it. Well, as I said, I picked Margaret up, hunted around for this wretched café, drove her home, then came back here. And just as I got to the gate, I saw Anne disappearing round the house to the back, so when I'd driven the car into the garage, I went round after her. In other words, I was only a minute or two behind her and I caught up with her just as she found Tom. She was holding on to the doorpost, beginning to sag at the knees. So I took her into the kitchen, then went to take a look at Tom. And I saw one of your pearl ear-rings lying beside him. So I went up to your bedroom and I saw your ivory box was empty. . . . Yes, I know," he went on, in response to a startled exclamation from Dr. Lindsay. " Only yesterday we were talking about the foolishness of keeping valuable jewels at home. Well, your priceless heirlooms are all gone—or else they're in Tom's pockets. I haven't looked, because I happened to remember that business about not touching anything on the scene of a murder. I suppose, by the way, you haven't been keeping me in the dark about possessing some diamond the size of a hen's egg, have you? "

" Don't be a fool," she said impatiently. " Anne, what happened to you? "

I was looking at Jess when Dr. Lindsay spoke to me. The poodle had followed us into the room and was sitting pressing herself against Peter's leg, with her head on his knee and her eyes fixed swimmingly on his face, as if she were following his story.

Lucky Jess, I thought. Nobody was going to question her. No one would force her to take difficult decisions concerning truth and falsehood. That was what was happening to me. There and then I had to decide whether

to tell the truth, the whole truth, or only some of it.
There was no need for me to tell a direct lie, but I had to
make up my mind whether or not to skip a little.

I skipped. I told Dr. Lindsay of how I had gone to the
bus stop and been picked up by Owen in the Jaguar;
how we had started towards Lachester, then turned
back because of the forgotten parcel of proofs, as a result
of which I had been a little late at the post office for my
appointment with Tom; how I had waited, then come
home by bus and found myself locked out; but in hopes
of finding an unfastened window, had gone round the
house and found the back door open and banging in the
wind. It was simple, so long as I didn't look at Peter.

" Oh, and there's one thing I'd forgotten," I added.
And then I stopped.

I had been going to tell Dr. Lindsay about seeing Geo.
Biggs's van in the lay-by between the bus stop and the
Loaders' house. But suppose Mr. Biggs, driving his van
into the lay-by a moment before Owen and I had driven
down the hill, had seen Peter and Jess in the garden. . . .

Dr. Lindsay hadn't noticed my sudden pause, because
just then a high, screaming bark of warning had come
from Jess. Bounding to the window, she tried to tell us,
in a hysteria of yelps, that we were about to be invaded
by a whole terrifying army of strangers. The police had
arrived.

I could easily have joined Jess in her hysteria. For
although it had been easy enough to do my little bit of
skipping, to say nothing about having seen Peter in the
garden at five minutes to three, or Mr. Biggs in the lay-by,
the thought of it was already a horrible load on my mind.
The thought that I had just supported Peter in the
stupidity of the lie that he had told to me and to Dr.
Lindsay, instead of forcing him, before he had become
disastrously committed to it, to tell us the truth about his
return to the house and what he had done after it, made

me feel that I should like to start banging my head against the wall. For I was as stupid as he was—even more stupid. I knew that I wasn't the only person who had seen Peter and Geo. Biggs. Owen had seen them. Almost certainly Owen had seen them.

CHAPTER IX

I HADN'T had time, at that point, to think about that lie of Peter's. I didn't know, I didn't even suspect, what it could mean. I wasn't afraid that it meant that he had murdered Tom. I wasn't even afraid yet that he knew who had. It was the mere fact of his having lied at all that scared me, with the thought that to lie at such a time was to put himself inevitably in danger.

Angry with both Peter and myself because of my fear, I went to my interview with Inspector Belden with a frightened feeling of our having already fatally missed our way on the only safe path.

Inspector Belden was a tall, solid man with sharp little grey eyes in a flat, red face to which fair, fluffy eyebrows and a wispy moustache clung like ferns in the crevices of a brick wall. He had an air of studied patience. But this didn't carry a great deal of conviction, for we had all heard him giving orders to the men who had come with him and I thought that he had a quick temper and that, in spite of the careful deliberation of his manner he would jump to conclusions as fast as anyone.

Between him and Dr. Lindsay there seemed to be a relationship of fractious trust. Both were strong-willed, dogmatic people and only a few minutes after they had gone together into the small room which Dr. Lindsay used as an office, and for interviewing the few patients who came to her home, both their voices could be heard,

raised in irritable argument. But when I was later called
into the room, the inspector looked determined to understand my point of view and make all allowances for me,
if it killed him.

It more nearly killed me. It was with a feeling of utter
exhaustion that at last I escaped from that room. I
must have told him at least three times who I was, where
I lived, where I worked, where and when I had met Peter,
all that I could remember of my meetings with Tom Hearn
and Sandra and Ivy May and of everything that had
happened during the afternoon. I told it all as faithfully
and fully as I could, except that I again skipped my glimpse
of Peter and Jess in the garden at five minutes to three,
and of Mr. Biggs in the lay-by. I found the skipping easier
than it had been the first time. Practice was making
perfect.

After Inspector Belden had finished with me, he saw
Peter, and then had another talk with Dr. Lindsay. Later
in the evening, when the photographers and the finger-
print men had gone, when Tom's body had been taken
away and a bleak sort of imitation normality had returned
to the house, Dr. Lindsay told Peter and me what she had
managed to make the inspector tell her during their second
interview. He had told her that Tom had got into the
house by climbing on to the roof of the garage, and from
there to an upper landing window, which had been left
open. Once inside, he had gone downstairs immediately
and opened the back door, as a get-away, in case he should
be surprised. He had then gone from one room to another
on the ground floor, looking for a drink. Because of the
rain his shoes had been wet and his movements had been
easy to follow. He had found the sherry decanter and had
drunk from it. Then he had gone upstairs and again gone
from room to room until he had found Dr. Lindsay's
bedroom, with the ivory box on her dressing-table.

He had not needed to break the box open, for there

had never been a key to it. He had simply emptied it into his pockets and there the police had presently found all that he had stolen, with the exception of the ear-ring which the Inspector thought Tom must still have been holding when a noise below had disturbed him, and which had dropped to the floor beside him when the shot had gone into him at the foot of the stairs.

He had been shot by someone standing in the kitchen doorway. Yet there were no wet footmarks there but Tom's, Peter's and my own, so the murderer must have taken the precaution of removing his shoes before entering the house. He had left, it seemed probable, on Tom's motor-bike, because there were marks in the garden, behind the hedge, to show where Tom had left it, but it was not there now. Finally, when the police arrived at half-past four, Tom had been dead between one and two hours.

As she finished telling us this, Dr. Lindsay went to the window, gave a sour glare at the people who had already gathered at the gate to stare in, and although it was still daylight, pulled the curtains together and switched on the light.

" That's better," she said, " though I suppose we're going to have to get used to that sort of thing in the next few days. Just why, I wonder, did he have to get himself murdered in my house? I've a busy enough life without that, haven't I ? "

She dropped into a chair and gave an exhausted yawn.

" There's one other thing Frank Belden told me," she said. " Your guesswork about Tom's occupation doesn't seem to have been so very wide of the mark. It's got to be checked in London, but Frank thinks Tom's a man with a record for the sort of thefts that have been happening round here. And there's been some suspicion that he was responsible for the Loader and the Milstrom burglaries, only at the time of the Milstrom burglary

he was seen by a number of witnesses in a pub in Paddington." She looked at Peter. " I gather you've told Belden
all about that."

" Yes," Peter said.

" Everything? "

" Yes."

" But it's puzzling why Tom came to my house, isn't
it? " she went on. " You wouldn't think I was in his
class. Apparently, though, he'd been slipping recently,
drinking too much and boasting. That's how he got
himself suspected of these recent jobs. Perhaps that's
why his gang decided to finish him off." She drummed
with her short, strong fingers on the arm of her chair.
" It *was* the gang, I suppose. And they did it here on
purpose to get you involved in it. For once, it's lucky
you ran into Margaret."

Peter stood up. " I think I'll ring her up," he said.
" I'd like to know if the police have been there yet to
check up what I told them about where I was."

" Wait a minute," she said. " The White Horse isn't
one of your usual haunts, is it, Peter? "

" I don't think I'd ever been in it before last Sunday,"
he said. " Are you wondering if that first meeting of
Anne's with Tom wasn't as chancy as it seemed? "

" Yes," she said.

" I've wondered about that too, but I think it must
have been. I stopped there on the impulse of the moment."

" But Margaret and Owen know it, don't they? "

" I'm not sure what you mean by that, but the truth
about them is that they know most of the pubs in the
neighbourhood pretty well." He went out. I heard a
tinkle as he picked up the telephone, and then the murmur
of his voice.

Dr. Lindsay turned to me. " Anne, have you ever
wondered if the way you met Tom and Sandra wasn't
completely accidental? "

I thought of Daniel Barfoot asking me almost the same question. But as he had asked it, it had suggested that Peter had been involved in whatever arrangements might have been made to bring about the meeting.

" Oh, I've wondered," I said. " I've also wondered why Sandra was so frightened that morning. At the time I thought she was just frightened at having to get on to Tom's motor-bike, when he was so obviously unfit to drive. But from what I've seen of her since, that doesn't seem to fit."

Dr. Lindsay gave a tired frown. " When did Sandra look frightened? "

" When she first saw me talking to Tom."

" You mean you think that, far from its being an arranged meeting, you weren't meant to meet each other."

" I don't know—perhaps."

She gave a wry smile. " Ah well, it's beyond me. I think I'd better get us something to eat. There's probably some cold meat and some salad in the fridge."

I was telling her that if she would tell me what she would like done, I would get the meal, when Peter came back into the room.

" Margaret and Owen will be here in a few minutes," he said. " The police have been to see them, to check up what Anne and I told them about our whereabouts, and they've just left and the Loaders were starting out to see us when I telephoned."

" Well, let's get that meal all the same," Dr. Lindsay said. " Come along, Anne, we'll get it together."

I suggested again that she should let me do it, but it seemed easier for her at the moment to do some of the work herself than to sit still. But when we had carried the cold roast beef and the bread and cheese into the dining-room the doorbell rang, so she left me to finish laying the table and hurried away to open the door, assuming that it was the Loaders arriving.

Instead, it was the first reporter on the scene. He was a local man, young, anxious and in a hurry, because he wanted to get the news away to some agency in London before anyone else arrived. Dr. Lindsay knew him slightly and dealt with him kindly but very firmly and managed to send him away without having let him discover the sensational fact that the dead man was the double of her adopted son.

After that there were more reporters, some at the door, some on the telephone and most of them a good deal more determined than the first, but once the Loaders arrived, Owen dealt with them, while Margaret sat with us in the dining-room. She refused to eat anything, saying that she and Owen had already had dinner, and she was more subdued than I had ever seen her. The haggardness of her face was startling. She barely glanced at Peter, but sat watching her own hands fiddling with a salt-cellar and a pepper-pot which were near her on the table.

When Dr. Lindsay shot some of her abrupt questions at her, Margaret corroborated Peter's story of his having seen her at the bus stop at a quarter to three, picked her up and taken her with him when he went to look for the café, then presently taken her home. She had also corroborated it, she told us, to the police, and Owen had told them about picking me up at the bus stop at this end and taking me into Lachester. As she said this she looked up at me with a dully puzzled stare, while her hands went on shifting the salt-cellar and pepper-pot as if they were pieces on a chess-board.

Dr. Lindsay had eaten her cold beef in a businesslike way. To eat was a task that she had set herself, but when she had finished she sat back in her chair with a little groan of fatigue.

"That's very useful, Margaret," she said. "My own belief, from his condition when I first saw him, is that Tom was shot not later than three o'clock—certainly

not much later. And it couldn't have been very much
earlier than that, because Anne and Mrs. Joy didn't
leave the house till about a quarter to three. So all the
members of our circle here seem to be pretty well covered
for the time that counts. I'm thankful for that. It's
liable to save us bother, if nothing more serious. I'm afraid
there'll be lots of bother, all the same, when this business
of Tom and Peter being twins hits the papers. What were
you doing at the bus stop, Margaret? "

Margaret was still watching me, so I saw how her
eyes widened at the question, and suddenly I wondered if
that steady gaze on my face was meant to warn me of
something. If so, it wasn't necessary. I had no intention
of questioning her story.

" Strangely enough, I was waiting for a bus," she
answered.

" Is that what you told the police—I mean, is that all
you told them? " Dr. Lindsay asked. , " Because you
don't usually use the buses, do you? "

" Not usually, but sometimes," Margaret said. " Owen
happened to want the car to-day. As a matter of
fact . . ."

" Yes? "

Margaret made a sharp move with the salt-cellar.
She might just have decided on a bold piece of play with
one of her bishops, although she was aware that this put
her queen in danger.

" As a matter of fact, Owen and I had a quarrel this
morning," she said. " We even talked of separating. And
to stop it, to give myself time to think, I simply ran out
of the house. I meant to go for a long walk, but the rain
was worse than I'd realised so when I saw a bus coming,
I got on to it and went to the White Horse and had a drink
and some sandwiches. That calmed me down and I went
to catch a bus home again and I was waiting for it when
Peter saw me. But of course I haven't told the police all

this. There's no reason why I should. I simply told them I went out for lunch and went by bus because Owen wanted the car."

" It seems to have been a morning for quarrels," Dr. Lindsay said gloomily.

Peter stood up so abruptly that his chair nearly fell over. He caught it and banged it back into place at the table. I thought he was going to say something violent, but he stopped himself and instead strode to the door. But before he reached it, it opened and Owen appeared, gesturing to someone whom we could not see to come into the room.

There was a pause, then high heels went click-clack on the floor of the hall and Sandra came in.

Just as she had when she came to my flat, she stood still only just inside the door, looking round with sullen caution before risking coming any farther. We had all got to our feet. From the way that she looked at us, we might have been a herd of cattle, of which she was frightened, but which she was forcing herself to encounter, as it blocked the road before her.

Owen came in after her and closed the door. At the sound she started slightly, shooting a furtive glance behind her. She was very changed since our last meeting. Her red hair was scraped back from her face into a pony-tail and was wet with the rain. Her make-up was streaked and caked by rain and tears. Her eyelids were swollen and her mouth was puffy. She looked very young and tragic and in frantic need of comfort and at the same time she looked dangerous. She looked as if the hands, which were thrust deep into the pockets of her waterproof, might reach out at any moment, with tearing nails, for somebody's face.

Peter was closest to her. He had stood still when she appeared, but now he took a step forward, meaning, I thought, to make some gesture of concern, take her

hand, perhaps, or put an arm about her shoulders. But
at once she cried out harshly, " Keep away from me!
Not that I care what you do, except that I'm going to
get you for what you did to Tom, that's all! That's what
I came to tell you. It won't help you making the cops
believe you didn't do it, because I'll be there—and I
know what happened."

Dr. Lindsay came forward. " You're Sandra May,
aren't you? " she said. " Take off your wet things, Sandra,
and sit down and let's talk this over quietly."

Sandra did not move. " I'm Sandra Hearn. I'm
Tom's wife. And I haven't come to talk anything over.
I've come to take a look at you all. I want to get your
faces into my mind so's I don't ever forget them. . . .
All right, I know Tom was a crook, but he never lifted
his hand against anyone to hurt them. He was soft, too
damned soft, if you want to know. Not like you! " Her
sullen stare settled on Peter's face. " But you won't get
away with it—oh no, Pete! Not with this you won't."

" Sandra, I didn't do it," he said. " I swear to you,
I didn't."

" Try that on the police," she said.

" I wasn't even here."

" Who says? "

" I do," Margaret said. " At the time Tom Hearn was
shot, Peter was with me the other side of Lachester."

" Yes, having been rung up," Peter added, " by your
mother—she really is your mother, isn't she, Sandra?—
who asked me to meet her at three o'clock at a place
called the Kettle on the Hob, which turned out not to
exist."

Sandra shook her head. " Mum never did that."

" She did," Peter said. " She seems to have wanted me
out of the way when Tom came here."

" If she'd been going to do that, I'd have known,"
Sandra said. " Like I knew Tom was coming here—all

right, I'm admitting all that, see? I always knew when
Tom was doing a job, because I had to try and keep him
sober for it. I said, you're crazy going to that place,
they won't have stuff worth your trouble, but he'd made
his mind up . . ." She stopped with a scared look, as if
she thought that this time she had said too much. But
then she shrugged. " I suppose he'd got information.
Tom generally worked on information received. And it
was Tom himself who rang up here to get Pete and Anne
out of the way—I know that because I was right there
beside him when he did it and he told me Pete had gone
out already, so we didn't have to worry about him. So
you can forget that story it was Mum rang Pete up.
Mum didn't shove her nose into Tom's business."

She started as Owen put a hand on her shoulder,
looking down with sympathy into her blotched face.

" My child, d'you know you're talking an awful lot
too much for your own good? " he said.

She jerked away from his hand and shrieked at him,
" D'you think I care? "

" Not now," he said. " Not to-day. But perhaps to-
morrow or the day after."

" What's it to you, anyway? " she asked suspiciously.

" Well, we're none of us here policemen," he said,
" but you're so young, I can't help feeling one of us
ought to tell you that what you're saying might get used
in evidence." He looked at Dr. Lindsay with rueful
apology. " It only seems fair, somehow . . ."

Stonily, she asked, " How did you hear of Tom's death,
Sandra? "

" How d'you think? " Sandra said. " I was waiting
for him. He didn't come. When I'd waited long enough,
I—I came here. There was a crowd at the gate. I heard
them talking. Then I saw them bring him out. . . ."
Her voice began to shake uncontrollably. She swung
round, groping blindly for the door-handle.

Owen shot out an arm and held the door shut. " Just
a minute. Where are you going now, Sandra? "

She leant her head hopelessly against the panelling of
the door. " What's it to you? "

" I'm not sure you're fit to go anywhere." He said.

" I'm all right," she said sullenly. " You let me go.
I've done what I came for."

" Will you take my advice? " he said. " Will you go
to the police now? Tell them what you've told us. I'll
drive you there, if you'll let me."

She answered with a hysterical giggle and grabbed
again at the door-handle.

" Let her go," Dr. Lindsay said.

At the words Sandra spun round again, her green
eyes ablaze, her drained, face coming alive with fury.

" I'm going, but don't think you're seeing the last of
me! " she shouted. She flung out a pointing finger at
Peter. " He's lying—and she's lying too! " The finger
swung towards Margaret. " If anyone telephoned him,
she did—not Mum. And if they were together, it was
here, that's where it was, where Tom found them. And
she——" The finger pointed at me. " She knows it.
I can see it in her face she knows it."

She wrenched the door open and ran out. A sharp
draught of cold air blew into the room as she tore the
front door open and let it slam behind her.

Owen gave a bemused shake of his head. He turned to
Margaret. But as he turned, his glance met mine and
was withdrawn so swiftly that from that moment I was
sure that Owen had both seen Peter in the garden here
at five minutes to three and seen and understood the
significance of Jess's friendly leaping up at him.

" Come along, Margaret," he said, " I think it's time
to go."

She shrugged her coat around her, as if she suddenly
felt cold.

" It isn't true, Anne," she said. " Peter saw me at the
bus stop near the White Horse at about two forty-five
and we were together in the car till he got to Long Grange
at half-past three or thereabouts."

" Come along," Owen repeated.

She went to his side and he put an arm through hers.

" I'll look in again in the morning, to see if there's
anything I can do," he said to Dr. Lindsay. " In any
case, call me if there's any way I can help."

" Thank you, Owen," she said. " I think I ought to
tell you now, however, since you seemed to sympathise
with that girl a good deal, that I'm going to call Frank
Belden about her now."

" Well, I suppose you must," he said. " Good night."

" Good night."

The Loaders went out together. Dr. Lindsay waited
a moment, then went with weary steps to the door. She
paused there and looked back.

" I'm quite sorry for her," she said defensively, as if
someone had just accused her of having failed in normal
pity. " But there's something about what's happened
that I think it's important not to forget. It is that there's
a sort of insanity in a burglar of Tom's class coming to
steal my jewellery. He's been so busy in his profession
lately—really so fantastically busy and so successful—
that he can hardly have been driven to come after my
stuff by need. And that suggests that all that girl's
remarkable admissions were lies and that Tom didn't
come here to steal, but for some quite different reason.
I don't know what. I don't know what at all. But I want
the police to know at least everything that I know.
Because, you see, on top of everything else . . ." She
thrust a hand through her white hair. " None of us has
said anything about it yet, but of course we've all been
thinking about it. Suppose it wasn't Tom who was meant
to be killed, but you, Peter. So there you are."

She trudged out down the hall to the telephone.

As she started to speak into it, Peter came to me, put his hands on my shoulders and forced me down into a chair. Bending my head back, he said in a soft, violent whisper. " Look at me, look at me! Stop looking right through me and tell me what I've done to you! "

CHAPTER X

HIS MERE TOUCH poured such reassurance into me that it didn't seem necessary to answer. It didn't seem necessary to think. If he would only go on holding me, it might with luck never be necessary to think again. This seemed absolutely clear to me for the moment. Clutching at him, I drew him down to me.

With a twist of his shoulders, he moved away.

" What have I done? " His features were rigid. " If you like, I'll say I was wrong this morning. I'll say I've been wrong ever since we ran into Tom. It was damned foolishness. I oughtn't to have bothered about him. I oughtn't to have gone to meet that woman to-day. I'll say anything you like. But what have I done to you that you look straight through me as if I wasn't here—and at a time like this ! Will you tell me that? "

I could hear Dr. Lindsay talking on the telephone in the hall, and I didn't want her to hear what I had to say to Peter. I answered in a whisper, " It was Jess. . . ."

He gave a loud, angry laugh. " What have I done to Jess? "

" Nothing—don't be silly. It was what Jess did."

" Silly? This is getting worse than insane," he said.

" Then tell me this," I said, " do you think Jess could tell the difference between you and Tom? "

" I don't know," he said. " I suppose so."

" She'd go by smell, wouldn't she, as much as by the look of you? "

" I should think so."

" If she met Tom, she'd know he was a stranger? "

" I imagine so."

" And she's frightened of strangers. She wouldn't rush up to a stranger in the garden and jump all around him with yelps of delight."

" No. Although . . ." The anger was fading from his face. I wasn't sure what to make of the expression that succeeded it. " She's such a crazy bitch, I wouldn't put it past her," he said cautiously. " When did you see her doing this? "

" At five to three, from Owen's car, as we drove down the hill from the Loaders' house after picking up his parcel."

" You mean you saw—me, let's say—in the garden here, with Jess jumping up at me? "

" Yes. And I'm afraid Owen and Mr. Biggs may have seen it too." I told him then about seeing Geo. Biggs's van in the lay-by.

" I see," Peter let a breath out slowly. " And so you haven't believed anything I've said about picking up Margaret at the bus stop."

" Explain it to me and I will," I said.

" I wonder if you will," he said. " I wonder if you want to, or are you looking for a way out? "

" Peter, that's a damnable thing to say," I said.

" Any more damnable than taking Jess's word against mine? "

That started me laughing. It was a helpless, hysterical laughter in which Peter, after a moment, joined.

Giggling stupidly, I said, " Poor, silly Jess! "

" Poor idiot Jess," Peter said, his shoulders shaking. " If she only knew! "

"Ah yes, if she knew she'd lie for you, wouldn't she?"

"No, no, she's honest, she's too stupid to lie." But as he said this, the laughter died out of his voice.

Mine stopped as suddenly and I became aware that it hadn't helped either of us. It had made things worse, because now we were both afraid of other, more dangerous feelings slipping out of control.

I got up and started to clear the table.

"I've told you what I saw," I said. "If it wasn't you, it was Tom. But if it was Tom, Jess was on excellent terms with him. And whichever of you it was, I'm sure Owen saw you too, whether or not Mr. Biggs did."

"How do you know that?" Peter asked.

"I saw it in his face."

He began helping me to clear the table. "You see too much in people's faces, Anne. And in dogs' faces."

"But you haven't explained how Jess knew Tom so well that she wasn't afraid of him," I said.

Peter let a handful of knives and forks drop on to a plate with a clatter. "God! . . . For all I know, Tom's been making up to her on the quiet, bringing her food, getting to know her. If he was getting ready to burgle this house, wouldn't that be a natural thing to do, particularly as he could wander around without attracting any attention, so long as Mother wasn't around and he was dressed more or less like me?"

I stood still, looking at him in astonishment. "I never thought of that."

"No, Anne, because you wanted to think the worst," he answered. "But that's the true explanation, I should think."

Yet there was a dubiousness in his tone which haunted me later, when I had gone up to bed and was lying there beside him, aching with tiredness but wide awake.

Why didn't Peter believe his own explanation, or why

had he thought that I couldn't believe it, I wanted to know, as I tossed and turned. What was the matter with it?

Between snatches of shallow sleep I went on trying to think it out and also trying to convince myself that I hadn't really heard that uncertainty in Peter's voice. With daylight creeping in at the window, I fell asleep and dreamt terrifyingly about white beads, long, long strings of them, that writhed about us, imprisoning and crushing us.

Next morning there were more reporters and more sightseers in the road. There was another visit from Inspector Belden and from some other detectives. Belden told us that Tom's motor cycle had been found in a car-park outside a cinema in Lachester. About half-way through the morning there was the visit from Owen which he had promised the evening before. By then Dr. Lindsay had gone out on her rounds, Peter had been shut up for the last half-hour with the inspector, and I was roaming the house, unable to keep still or to find any adequate reason for doing anything useful. For the longer Peter's interview with the police went on, the more it tore at my nerves, while the glimpses that I had from the windows, as I wandered aimlessly about, of all the avid faces at the gate, made me so frantic that if I had chanced on the undiscovered murder-weapon, as some of the newspapers had called it, I felt as if I might have started shooting.

In the circumstances, Owen's solid figure in the doorway of the sitting-room, where I happened at that moment to be looking unsuccessfully for cigarettes, his ruddy, good-humoured face, flat little nose and sun-bleached hair, were a welcome and steadying sight.

" Here you are," he said, realising what I was looking for and holding out cigarettes to me. " Better keep the packet. The rate of consumption in the household has probably gone up since yesterday. I'll get some more on my way home." He brought his lighter out of his pocket. "Where's Peter?"

I gestured towards Dr. Lindsay's office. "In there with the police. I don't know what they think they can get out of him to-day that they didn't get out of him yesterday."

"Perhaps they've been checking his alibi and want to go over it all again with him," Owen suggested. Turning away to the window, he stood there, glowering at the gate. "The human race," he remarked disgustedly.

I sat down stiffly, watching him until he turned back to look at me again, then I said, "Do you think there's anything the matter with that alibi, Owen?"

I thought he would probably laugh the suggestion off, but instead he crossed to the door, made sure that it was closed, then came back and sat down near me.

"Look, Anne," he said in a low voice, "we both know Peter came back long before he said he did. I know you saw him, because it was your exclamation that made me look in this direction and see him too—Peter with Jess. That's the point, isn't it? He was playing with Jess. So it wasn't Tom. I'm not beating about the bush, because I know you know that. I saw it in your face last night, when Peter and Margaret were telling their stories. So Peter's alibi has very likely faded into thin air by now. Police bring that sort of thing about quite easily."

"Are you trying to say *you've* told them . . . ?"

"No," he said. "There's no need for either of us to say anything about it, is there? We may be the only people who understand what we saw. But George Biggs was there—d'you remember? He may have seen Peter."

"Have you told the police about seeing George Biggs?" I asked.

"No," he said.

I tossed the cigarette I had barely started to smoke into the empty fireplace. "Well, d'you know something,

Owen? It wasn't Peter in the garden. I told him what we'd seen and his explanation was so simple I felt an awful fool for ever having suspected anything else."

" If the explanation was very simple and satisfying, it was probably Margaret's idea," Owen said. " She was a quite promising journalist before she married and she's got a first rate talent for putting together a clear and convincing story out of fairly slender materials. Sad to say, it's been going entirely to waste for the last year, and I sometimes think that's what's the matter with her. Only between you and me, she's not so very keen on hard work."

" Will you listen to me and stop having evil thoughts," I said. " That wasn't Peter we saw, it was Tom."

" You know, Anne, you had evil thoughts well in advance of me," he said. " Or if that isn't entirely true, it was you who roused mine from their comfortable dormant state."

" If that's true, I'm sorry—very sorry," I said. " Because, don't you see, if Tom wanted to burgle this house, it was natural for him to make friends with Jess first, wasn't it? "

" If he could," Owen said. " I've been trying to make friends with Jess ever since I came here, without any success whatever."

" She might have been prejudiced in Tom's favour, because of his looking so like Peter," I said. " I don't know about that, but anyway, it's obviously what happened."

" Not obviously at all," he said, " because it's far from obvious that Tom came here to burgle the house. Dr. Lindsay's jewellery may be very pretty and precious to her, but as Sandra put it, it wasn't really worth Tom's trouble. So if by any chance it was Tom we saw with Jess, I'll tell you what I think that would most probably mean— and I'm not sure that you'll find this thought any more comforting than the thought that it was Peter. I think it would mean that Jess was friends with Tom because she'd met him before with Peter, perhaps met him quite often. And that would mean, you see, that Tom and Peter knew one another before Peter said anything about Tom to you or Dr. Lindsay."

There was Daniel Barfoot's suggestion coming up again in another form. I began to feel angrily entangled in the argument. At the same time my worries of the night came back to me, my feeling that Peter himself hadn't believed what he'd suggested about Tom's making friends with Jess because he was getting ready to burgle the house.

" Well, why *did* Tom come here, if it wasn't to burgle the house? " I demanded. " After all, he did come, didn't he? "

" Yes, he came," Owen agreed sombrely.

" And he'd made certain the house would be empty before he came."

" Yes."

" So what was he trying to do? "

" I can't think, Anne. So you may be right. I hope you are, because it's the most comfortable explanation for you and me. Everyone's been telling us the truth and nothing but the truth and we've nothing to worry about—except, of course, who murdered Tom and why."

" Dr. Lindsay suggested he was murdered because someone mistook him for Peter," I said. " What do you think of that, Owen? "

He took a moment to answer, then he said, " What am I supposed to think, Anne? That you believe I did the murder out of jealousy? Or was it Margaret? "

As I felt my face go red, he laughed.

" It's wonderful what a little unhappiness does to a nice person," he said. " I'm sure you aren't normally as malicious as that."

" I didn't think I was being any more malicious than you," I said.

" No—perhaps I'm the malicious one," he agreed unexpectedly readily. " Or rather worse than malicious. I'm sorry, Anne. Worms shouldn't turn, I'm afraid. The unaccustomed effort makes them lose their sense of proportion. Honestly, I haven't meant to attack Peter, though that's what it sounded like, I expect." He got up and went to the window. " I've been talking far too much. And I'm not a good person to listen to. Not for you. My mind's too full of suspicions—dull and tired with them."

" I'm beginning to think it's time I told you not to worry so much about what doesn't mean anything," I said. " You were telling me that yesterday, but you seem to have forgotten it."

Gazing out, he said absently, " I wonder if I ever really believed it."

" Oh, Owen! "

" Do you believe it, Anne? Oh, don't answer. I know you want to believe it. So do I—I suppose." He turned his back to the window and looked at me again. " Unless I've stopped wanting it. I'm not sure any more. Until last night I knew what I wanted—I thought I knew. But now . . ."

" Why last night? " I asked.

" It was listening to them both lie, so harmoniously, so—so damned intimately," he said. " Is there anything more intimate, I'd like to know, than two people telling the same lie, without even having to look at each other to make sure they're getting it right? I think I gave up then, and then suddenly realised that it was a relief to give up."

" I haven't given up," I said.

" Last night you were nearer to it than I was."

" Because I thought they really were telling lies," I

admitted. "Now I don't think so. I think there's a perfectly simple explanation of what we saw. And I feel ashamed of the way I jumped to the conclusion that they were lying, simply because I saw that ridiculous dog, who very likely hasn't even got a sense of smell at all, which would account for her general mental deficiency, wouldn't it? I mean a dog with no sense of smell would be like a human being with a lobe of his brain missing— and of course she wouldn't be able to distinguish between Peter and Tom. . . ."

This new unconvincing argument poured out of me. I clung to it as if I were clinging to Peter. And in the middle of it I realised that the door had quietly opened and that Peter was standing there, listening to me, while Jess, behind him, poking a quivering nose past him, seemed to be listening too.

Sounds in the garden suggested that the police had left the house.

" It's no good," Peter said as I stopped. " It's a very rum position to be in, but sooner or later I'm going to be forced by sheer logic to admit that I was in two places at the same time. Like that fellow Geo. Biggs told us about, the one who was seen in London and in India at the same time—do you remember? Geo. Biggs thought he had a second self wandering about out of control. Well, I must have a second self wandering about most horribly out of control."

He had come into the room while he was talking, but Jess, after a distrustful look at Owen, had pattered off down the hall to the safe familiarity of Mrs. Joy's company in the kitchen.

" I hope you didn't say anything about that to the police," Owen said.

" No, they don't seem to have caught on to the fact yet that I'm supposed to have been seen here," Peter said. " I ought to thank both of you for kindly keeping this apparition to yourselves. I'm very grateful. If you hadn't, I believe I'd find myself not merely in a rum position, but a very nasty one." He was speaking lightly, but there was a tautness about him which made me wonder what he was holding in. In a moment I knew. " Mum, you see, my dear, devoted Mum, has sworn to the police that she never telephoned me yesterday morning, and a friend who spent the morning with her also swears she never went near any telephone. So bang goes that part of my alibi, unless someone remembers my asking them for the Kettle on the Hob."

" Some of your alibi is still intact, however—the part of it that Margaret gave you," Owen said stiffly.

" That—oh yes," Peter said.

" Then why worry? "

There was a slight pause, then Peter gave a shrug, as if to dismiss the matter.

" I've decided to go to London to have a talk with Mum," he said. " Are you coming with me, Anne? Belden says we can go if we want to."

CHAPTER XI

THE POLICE were still in the garden when Peter and I came out of the house and when we got into the car they obligingly shooed the crowd away from the gate. But as we drove off, I couldn't get the thought of those watching faces out of my head. Who were those people? Where had they come from? How would they normally have been spending their Sunday morning if they hadn't heard that there had been a murder in Dr. Lindsay's house?

Individually they looked quite ordinary people, not noticeably morbid, cruel or even excessively stupid. They

had the sort of faces you see everywhere around you
without any shocked feeling that you will probably
remember them for the rest of your life. But in a crowd,
even that small, patient, quiet crowd, they became
something hauntingly horrible.

" Can you understand them at all? " I said to Peter as
we got clear of them and started on the road to Lachester.

" Probably can't read and the telly's out of order," he
said. " I shouldn't worry about them."

" They make me think of the crowds at Tyburn."

" Well, the crowds at Tyburn couldn't read and hadn't
got the telly either."

" They're a good reason, all by themselves, for going to
London," I said. " But this idea of yours of talking to
Ivy May, Peter . . ."

" Well? "

" You don't really think she'll tell you anything, do
you? "

" Probably not."

" Then why are we going? "

" Don't you want to go? " he said. " We can go back,
if you want to."

" No, I don't want to do that."

" Then we might as well go on." He was still talking
in that light, unnatural way which made me feel as if there
were a sheet of thick glass between us.

" Oh, Peter, please tell me what you're up to! " I
said. " Do you think you can make Ivy May tell you
something she wouldn't tell the police? "

" Who knows? " he said.

" How do you mean to set about it? "

" Perhaps I can manage to frighten her more than the
police have."

" Well, if you won't tell me . . ."

After a moment he said, " It's odd, I seem to have lost
the knack of making you believe anything I say."

"I'm sorry, but I can't see you setting out deliberately to frighten anybody," I said.

"You'll see it presently, then."

"I'll believe it when I see it."

"All right then, wait and see. You'll see that second self of mine go into action." He paused again, narrowing his eyes against a beam of sunshine that broke through the clouds, making the roadway, still wet from yesterday's rain, glitter with small rainbows. "As a matter of fact, there's something else besides the telephone call that I want to see that woman about. You remember what you were telling Owen about Jess possibly having no sense of smell?"

"Yes," I said.

"Well, you know that's nonsense, don't you?"

"Is it?"

"Of course it is. It would be quite easy to prove her sense of smell was normal."

"Oh, let's stop bothering about Jess!" I said explosively. "Owen isn't going to say anything to the police about seeing her and nor am I, and if Biggs saw anything he probably didn't understand it—so let's forget her."

A muscle began to twitch in Peter's cheek. "There's got to be an explanation of what you saw."

"And you're going to beat it out of Mum somehow? Have you got your knuckle-dusters?"

I was goading him, of course, and I couldn't stop it. I wanted him to lose his temper, to come out from behind that sheet of glass.

But though the muscle in his cheek still twitched, his voice stayed level. "One possible explanation is that it wasn't Jess you saw. If you couldn't tell the difference between Tom and me, I don't see how you could tell the difference between Jess and another poodle. And another poodle is one of the things I'm going looking for now—or traces of another poodle. I'll look in Ivy May's flat and I'll look in Sandra's, if I can get the address of it out of her mother."

I turned that over in my mind before answering him. We were in the narrow main street of Lachester, almost empty of traffic to-day because it was Sunday. We passed the closed-up post office where yesterday I had waited vainly for Tom.

" Are you serious? " I asked.

" Perfectly serious."

" The only thing is . . ."

" What? "

" Oh, never mind," I said. " I'll go looking for a dog's hairs while you're busy frightening Ivy May."

" Will you do just that, Anne? "

I promised him that I would. But I couldn't see any-thing better about the idea of a second poodle than about the idea that Tom had troubled to make friends secretly with Jess before going to burgle Dr. Lindsay's house. Both would have meant that he had gone to a lot of trouble over an insignificant burglary. Unless, of course, his reason for having a poodle with him had been perfectly innocent and not part of an elaborate preparation for an insignificant burglary. It wasn't impossible that Tom had just happened to like poodles. Somewhere in the embryo which had divided to produce Tom and Peter there might have been an inherited liking for poodles. A poodle-loving gene, as well as a rock-climbing, house-climbing gene. I wished I could believe in it.

Yet I vaguely remembered that astonishing similarities had been found in later life between twins separated at birth. For instance, hadn't there been one pair some-where in America who had ended up both as electrical engineers, or something like that, and actually working in different branches of the same company?

I thought that that was something which Daniel

Barfoot would probably be able to tell me all about. It was just the kind of thing about which he was likely to have a store of information. I wished suddenly that I could see him. He would help me to get back the sense of reality which I had lost sometime the day before.

We had just passed the White Horse when I said to Peter, "There's something I'd like to do before we go back to Lachester, Peter. When we've finished with Mum, could we go out to Hendon to see my friends, the Barfoots?"

Peter said he supposed we could, but I saw that his mind hadn't been on my question or his answer.

We had a quick lunch of sandwiches and tea at a café and arrived at the mews where Ivy May lived at about half-past two. The day had been growing hotter and because of all the rain of the last day or two the air was heavy and the mews had a smell of damp soot and petrol fumes.

Peter rang the bell beside the lilac-painted door, from which the card with the name Hearn on it had disappeared. One of the small windows above us opened and Ivy May looked out. Whoever it was that she had been expecting, it hadn't been Peter and me. A hand went to her mouth and she slammed the window down again.

"Perhaps we don't get let in," I said.

And for a moment nothing more happened. But then we heard her feet on the stairs inside and she opened the door, dragging at the zip of her skirt to fasten it. It was a very short and full black-and-white striped skirt, which she was wearing with an emerald-green blouse, and it made her look more than ever like Sandra, except that the artless, cheerful excitement on her face was as unlike the anguished ferocity that we had seen last night on her daughter's as it could have been. Tom Hearn, I thought, had never meant anything to Ivy.

"Sorry to keep you, my dears, but I was just having

a lie-down when you rang," she said, " and I had to throw on a thing or two. And what a turn it gave me, seeing you, Peter. It was as if poor Tom himself was standing there. Come along up. Yes, poor old Tom! "

She turned and went up the stairs.

" Nice of you to call again," she said. " That girl of mine's broken to pieces over Tom and I'm absolutely worn-out, trying to cheer her up. But mind you, I've always said to her Tom would turn out badly. ' Look at the way he's drinking,' I said. ' Once they start that, they never stop. It's no good thinking,' I said, ' you'll be able to pull him up. The love of a good woman is about as much good for that job as one of the toy boats you see the kids sailing on the pond in the park'd be for crossing the Atlantic.' But would she listen? Not a hope! She's like me, poor girl. When she loves a man, she doesn't worry about his character, she just gives him all she's got." Sighing heavily, she took us into the room where we had sat before.

It was dirtier and untidier than it had been then, with some beer-bottles and used glasses on the hearth, a lot of newspapers scattered about the chairs, a pair of shoes and some stockings in the middle of the floor, all the ash-trays overflowing and a layer of greasy London dust over everything. On that other afternoon, I thought, when Peter had been welcomed into the place as a long-lost son, some attempt must have been made to tidy up, which it would have been far too great an effort to continue.

" Sorry about the mess," Ivy May went on, bundling newspapers together so that we could sit down. " Sandra brought all these in this morning. ' Look,' I said, ' that isn't going to do you any good. You'd far better try to get your mind off it,' I said. ' I know what you're going through, dear, don't think I don't, but you haven't stopped crying all night and that's bad for you and it's doing poor old Tom no manner of good, you may be

sure, and it's sending me up the wall. Will you stop it! '
I said. Well, of course, she didn't—not a hope! "

She was talking in a quick, fluttery way, moving her
hands a great deal and smiling at us with her girlish
brightness all the time. She would have gone on too, for
any length of time, if it could have stopped us talking.
But at that point Peter asked, " Is Sandra here? "

" Oh, is it Sandra you want, dear? " she said hopefully.
" I'd have told you right away if I'd known—she's out.
And I don't know when she'll be back."

" No, we don't want Sandra," Peter said. " It was
you we came to see."

" Well now, if it's about our little joke on you, Peter,"
she ran on, " the time you and Anne came before—well,
you aren't going to be hard on me about it, are you?
It was poor old Tom's idea. I said to him, ' But it isn't
really right, Tom,' I said, ' pretending to be his mother.
You don't know what feelings he may have about his
mother,' I said. ' And at my age too—what *will* he
think of me? ' ' Never you mind,' Tom said, ' it'll be a
laugh. You're a wonderful actress, Ivy,' he said, ' I can't
wait to see you.' And that was the trouble, dear. I never
can resist a chance to do a little bit of acting. It's born
in me. It was meant to be my life, only what with one
thing and another and having Sandra to take care of,
I never seemed to get going, somehow."

" All right, we can forget about that joke," Peter said.
" But what I do want to know, Mrs. May——"

" Call me Ivy, dear."

" What I want to know," Peter said, " is why you told
the police you didn't telephone me yesterday morning."

" Oh, that! " To my surprise, she looked relieved.
" But I didn't phone you—that's why I told them that.
Would you sooner I told them something else? Just tell
me what you want me to say——"

" Mrs. May, I want you to tell them the truth about

having telephoned me yesterday and asked me to meet you at a café called the Kettle on the Hob," Peter said.

"Oh, I can't say that *now*," she said in a tone of distress, "because I've already told them I didn't, and if I change it now, they'll know I'm lying and it won't do you any good any more than me. Of course, if I'd known sooner . . ."

"You did telephone me," Peter said.

She shook her head. "No, dear."

He went on patiently, "I recognised your voice, Mrs. May."

"No, dear. I don't know who it could have been, but it wasn't me." With her fair hair swinging, she turned to me. "Did you hear this person, Anne, who said she was me?"

Peter answered. "You know she didn't. You only spoke to me."

"Well, it's a puzzle," she said, resting a cheek on one hand. "I mean, if someone really did say to you it was me. Because it couldn't have been me—I can prove it. And that's what I said to the police. 'I can prove it,' I said. 'You look round this place,' I said, 'and you'll soon see there isn't a telephone. And I never went out at all yesterday till after I'd had my lunch, and I had it late like I always do,' I said, 'about two o'clock. And my friend Mrs. Barry spent the morning here, as she'll tell you, using my iron to press some blouses and a couple of evening dresses, because her iron had fused. Look round,' I said. And you may be sure they did. The way they looked, you'd have thought they expected me to keep a telephone hidden up the chimney. Well now, if you want to, you look round too, Peter dear, because I don't like to see you looking so worried."

He got up at once and went out.

I thought that it surprised Ivy May that he had

E

accepted her invitation to look round so promptly, but she gave a good-humoured shrug of her shoulders.

" Honest, Anne, I never phoned him," she said.

" Then I suppose it was Sandra, pretending to be you," I said.

" Sandra? " she said sharply. The guileless eyes suddenly weren't guileless at all, but pin-point sharp.

" Her voice is very like yours," I said. " It would have been easy for her to say she was you."

It was odd to watch her trying to work out whether or not it would be useful to agree with me. She couldn't really think fast. She could only elaborate fast a story she had prepared beforehand, or had had prepared for her by somebody else.

At last she shook her head. She shook it several times, with increasing emphasis.

" It wasn't Sandra. She was with Tom when he tried to phone Peter. But have you thought about its being this woman he says he picked up at the bus stop? "

" She couldn't imitate your voice, Mrs. May," I said. " She's never met you."

" I didn't say she imitated my voice. It was Peter said she'd my voice. Still I don't want to start putting ideas in your head."

" What I can't understand is why you should be afraid to admit it was you who telephoned," I said.

" Because I *didn't*! " Her voice went up a little.

" You could always say you changed your mind about going to meet him. Your friend Mrs. Barry could corroborate that for you, couldn't she? "

She pressed her hands together. " But I didn't, Anne! How can I get you to believe me? Look—I never knew properly what Tom was up to. I was fond of him in a way—you couldn't help it, really. He was a good-natured fellow and generous with his cash, when he had it and always good-humoured as long as he was sober. But

I never liked what he'd done to Sandra. I never did. She worshipped the ground he walked on—the ground he walked on even a week ago! She was crazy about him. And I didn't like it."

, A roughness had come into her voice which gave it an unfamiliar note of sincerity.

" Where's Sandra now? " I asked.

A dark flush of anger flowed over her face.

" She's with the police—that's where! Ever since ten o'clock this morning. They came and fetched her in a car and they've kept her ever since. Threatening her, shining lights in her eyes, letting her go hungry and thirsty—that's what Tom brought her to. My Sandra. I did what I could for that boy, because there was something about him—I can see it in your fellow too—that got round you so you couldn't believe he was really bad. And I'm nothing much myself, so I'm not one to cast stones. But when I think of what he brought my Sandra to——! "

There was a shriek in the passage. It was a shriek of mortal terror, the sort of sound that is torn unconsciously out of a human throat and that leaves behind no memory in the mind of the screamer but of pain and darkness. It was an animal sound which set my nerves tingling with primitive panic.

As I sprang up, I heard Peter saying apologetically, " Oh, Sandra—I'm so sorry—it's only me."

There was another shriek then, but this time it was of rage and there was a rush of feet in the passage. Ivy May and I collided as we ran to the door. Peter was out there, with Sandra struggling like a madwoman in his arms. He had her arms pinned to her sides, but at the end of them her fingers were curving convulsively, with long nails ready to tear at his face if she could free herself.

Her mother strode up to her and slapped her hard in the face.

Sandra screamed again, that scream of hatred and rage. There was no terror now in her blotched face, but only plain and simple murder.

" You stop that! " Ivy shrieked at her and slapped her again.

" Oh, for God's sake——! " Peter said. " Both of you stop it! "

A shiver went through Sandra. She gave a little moan and went limp in his arms. If he hadn't held on to her she would have flopped to the floor. Half lifting, half dragging her, he took her into the sitting-room and thrust her into a chair.

She remained there collapsed, in her dirty white cotton waterproof, with her red hair falling unkempt on to her shoulders, as if all the life had drained out of her angular young body and her mind had gone vacant. Only her eyes did not close, but followed Peter with dull watchfulness as he moved away from her.

He said unhappily to Ivy, " She didn't expect me and she thought she was seeing Tom. I think she could do with some brandy."

Ivy took hold of the girl's shoulder and shook her. " Sandra—Sandra, are you all right, love? "

" Let me alone," Sandra muttered.

" But are you all right? What did the police do to you? " Ivy looked up at me. " It's like I said, they've kept her all this time, giving her nothing to eat or drink, shining lights in her eyes—— "

" Shut up! " Sandra said. " They gave me tea and sandwiches. I don't care about the police. It's—it's—it's him. . . ."

She looked as if she were going to shoot up out of her chair and launch herself again at Peter. But she didn't seem to have the strength in her body now to lift herself. She let her head drop forward on to her chest and tears slithered down her cheeks.

" We'd better be going," Peter said. " Is Sandra living here with you now, Mrs. May? "

" Of course she is, poor kid," Ivy said. " Where d'you think she'd be living? "

" Has she given up the place she had with Tom? "

Ivy had turned to a cupboard and was taking out a bottle of whisky. " Oh yes," she said. " Don't go yet, Pete. Stay and have a drink. Don't worry about Sandra. It's just the shock and her being worn-out. She doesn't mean you any harm."

" What's happened to the dog? " Peter said.

If he meant it as shock-tactics, he met with no success whatever. Ivy only gave him a puzzled stare before she started pouring whisky into one of the glasses that she picked up off the floor.

" Didn't Sandra and Tom have a dog? " Peter asked.

Sandra came up groggily out of her chair, but it was not to attack Peter again. Frowning at the ground as if it were heaving under her, she went out of the room, then we heard the clatter of her heels on the stairs as she stumbled down them.

Ivy ran out after her, calling, " Sandra, come back! You're not to go out! "

But the door downstairs banged and uneven footsteps went tapping away over the cobbles.

Ivy came back and drank thirstily from the glass that she was holding.

" Well, what a life! " she said.

" We'd better be going," Peter repeated and, taking hold of my arm, drew me to the door.

" It was nice to see you again, dear," Ivy May said absently as we went out.

We were some way from the lilac-coloured door before I said to Peter, " I didn't notice the knuckle-dusters."

He didn't seem to hear me.

" I didn't notice any dog's hairs either," I said.

A little farther on I said, " What kept you so long, hunting round the flat? "

This time, starting the car, he answered, " Looking for anything that would help, but I didn't find anything. Now let's go back to the flat, Anne. I want to talk to you."

I was glad to go back to the flat. The two nights that I had been away from it felt like two months, two months spent in a strange, foreign land in which all the customs were different from any that I had ever known before. But as Peter and I climbed the stairs to it and I opened the door, I found that the strangeness had followed us, or was inside us, and that it came in with us.

It smelt hot and musty in the flat, so I went round, opening the windows, while Peter stood absently turning over some of the scattered pages of notes for his thesis, which were speckled already with black London dust, as if we had really been away for a long time. As I came back into the sitting-room from the kitchen, he looked up at me. Until that moment I hadn't noticed how sharp his features had become, as if the flesh had been drawn tighter over the bone behind.

" Well now, let's sort things out," he began abruptly. " We're going to suppose I've been lying to you. We're going to suppose it was me you saw in the garden yesterday afternoon. We're going to suppose——"

" We aren't going to suppose anything of the kind," I interrupted, going to him and putting my arms round him, feeling that this also was something that I hadn't done for so long that I hardly remembered what it felt like.

" Wait a minute," he said, moving back out of my reach. " We're going to suppose, for purposes of argument, just what I've said. That I lied to you about its not being me you saw in the garden. That I lied to

you about its being Ivy May who rang me up and asked
me to meet her. And let's say Margaret's been lying with
me. With me and for me. All right then—what do you
feel about it? "

" I don't feel anything about it," I said.

" Oh yes, you do."

" I do not, because it isn't so," I said.

The muscle in his cheek started twitching again. " But
you do think it's so, don't you, Anne? "

" I don't."

" And I can't prove that it isn't, can I ? " he said. " I
can't explain Jess's queer behaviour with Tom. And you
can bet I shan't be able to break Ivy May's alibi for
that telephone call. So there you are! Is that something
you can live with? "

" Oh, Peter——"

" No, no," he said, " this is important. I don't know
what you believe about that telephone call. Perhaps you
aren't really inclined to trust Ivy's friend Mrs. Barry as
implicitly as Jess. But you do trust Jess. And so do I and
I believe you saw what you said you saw, although I
can't explain it."

" Let's not try to explain it," I said. " It doesn't
matter."

" Because Owen and you have both decided not to
mention it to the police? That isn't the problem between
you and me."

" No, but—but I *don't* think it was you I saw," I said.

In a gentle, almost indulgent tone, he said, " Only I
think you do really, Anne darling, or if you don't at the
moment, it's because Margaret's fifty miles away, and
you'll suddenly find yourself believing it again when
next you catch sight of her and me together. So I think
for the moment I'm going off on my own to see if I can
find that other poodle. I found an address in Ivy's flat
that I think was Sandra's and Tom's, and even if the dog's

dead now, like Tom, the people there may have seen it sometime. I'll visit your friends the Barfoots with you some other time."

While he had been speaking, he had been moving towards the door.

As I said, " Don't, Peter—don't go! " he opened it and went out. There was sharp, unexpected violence in the way that he let it slam behind him.

I ran after him, but by the time that I had the door open again he was out of sight down the stairs.

I stood there stupidly for a moment, trying to decide how bad a thing had happened to us. With a sinking of the stomach, I felt that it might be a very bad thing indeed and that perhaps I should never see him again. But I was too much taken by surprise to know if this was a real feeling, a real fear. Automatically, I turned back into the flat, letting the door shut behind me. Then I went quickly out on to the landing again and down the flight of stairs to the half-landing below, from the window of which I could see the street. I had some idea that from the way Peter walked as he came out of the building, from the way that he got into the car and drove off, I might be able to guess what was really in his heart just then.

I waited, watching. I could see the car parked beside the pavement a little way down the street, so I knew that he hadn't been too quick for me and gone during the moment when I had returned to the flat.

How long I waited before I realised, with a start, that he was taking altogether too long to reach the street, I don't know. I had seen two other men come out, get into a car and drive away. But Peter appeared to have stayed loitering somewhere below. Perhaps, I thought hopefully, he was changing his mind, deciding to come back and either give up the hunt for that imaginary dog, or else take me with him.

I went running down the stairs to meet him.

On the half-landing two floors down, I found him, slumped in the corner, with blood all over his face, unconscious.

CHAPTER XII

I MUST HAVE screamed, because one of the doors on the landing immediately opened and by the time that I had got down the remaining stairs to where Peter lay, the woman who lived behind the door was out on the landing, looking down at me and calling, " Don't move him—don't move him! "

For the last two years she and I had been passing on the stairs, saying good morning and good evening and wasn't it a nice day. She was one of those indistinct women of about fifty who slip in and out of their burrows unnoticed, appear to have no friends and to leave no traces of themselves when they pass. Then one day you learn from somebody else that they run huge offices practically single-handed with enormous efficiency and if some chance crisis reveals their talents to you, they turn out to have intelligence, energy and their own kind of unexpected charm.

Miss Perry was very efficient now. It was she who brought the ambulance and, seeing me standing about, looking dazed and helpless, sent me upstairs to pack a bag to take to the hospital for Peter. She kept the other tenants at bay too, not without a certain air of triumph in having been the first on the spot and so the one who had the right to put herself between them and the interesting things that were going on, but it was all with a brisk determination for which I was immeasurably grateful.

I was grateful also that there was no melodrama about

her. She had not seen the two men whom I had seen from the window above come out of the block of flats and go to their car and so she took for granted that Peter had simply slipped on the stairs and fallen. If she had had the faintest suspicion that anything else had happened, she would have insisted on sending at once for the police. I meant to do this shortly myself, but just then I did not want to have them arriving, starting their questioning, getting in touch with Inspector Belden in Lachester, no doubt, and so probably getting in the way of my going to the hospital with Peter.

Going upstairs to pack the bag, however, I couldn't concentrate on what I was doing, for I was still stupid with shock, and my hands and brain fumbled helplessly with the problems of packing. I couldn't decide which bag to take and when I realised that Peter's razor, toothbrush, dressing-gown and slippers were all in Lachester, I stood looking round blankly, as if I thought that if I gazed hard enough at an empty shelf or peg, these things would materialise there.

At last, when the fog in my mind cleared a little, I dumped the zip bag which I sometimes used for shopping on the bed, and put into it some old slippers of Peter's, which I saw at the back of a cupboard and an old silk dressing-gown, which he hardly ever wore, because he was more attached to a still more ancient one. Then I opened the drawer where, with luck, I thought, I should find a clean pair of pyjamas.

Inside was a crumpled tumble of shirts and pants which was the normal result of his having done his own packing to go to Lachester. In the midst of it I found the pyjamas, but also I found something else, at sight of which I drew my hand back as if it had been a snake that I had touched, coiled up amongst Peter's underclothes. It was a gold chain, tangled up with a bracelet and a few rings and some other things. I didn't investigate what they were.

Slamming the drawer shut, panting, I looked over my shoulder.

There was no one there. There was no one but me in the flat. It was all right. But I had to nerve myself to open that drawer again as if the handles were red-hot.

I don't know what I should have done next if I had had time to think. But with Peter on the stretcher in the ambulance and the men waiting for me, ready to go, there seemed to be nothing to do but scoop up that handful of jewellery, drop it into the bottom of my handbag, put the pyjamas into the zip bag and go running downstairs.

For the next hour I hardly thought about the jewellery. Yet after I had filled in some of the usual forms at the hospital, I had nothing to do but sit in the waiting-room, wait, wonder, hope and fear. Still, I could no more think about my extraordinary find than I could think about calling the police. The two things seemed to cancel each other out. If I tried to think about one of them, the shadow of the other spread over it and blotted it from my mind. But I never stopped being conscious of what was in my handbag. The bag itself seemed to have become pounds heavier than it really was, a dead weight, dragging on my arm.

The chair in the waiting-room was small and very hard and although the summer evening was warm, there seemed to be a chill in the room, which set me shivering. Another woman there started to talk to me in a soft, desperate monotone. I did not take in what she said and I began to feel a sort of hatred of her, because she wouldn't leave me in peace to endure the bewildering blankness of my mind. Then I caught sight of her eyes and hated myself and at least tried to look as if I were listening. But it was a relief when a nurse came to fetch her from the room.

Presently a nurse came to me and told me that the doctor wanted to see me. He was a young man, whose off-hand air of self-importance irritated me, though to some extent he reassured me. He said he didn't think there was anything much the matter with Peter, but that they would keep him there at least for the night, checking his pulse and his temperature, in case of unpleasant developments. There was no need for me to stay, he said. I answered that I should prefer to stay for a while.

He nodded and then asked me how it had happened.

" He fell downstairs," I said, aware that he was watching me far too casually for it to be natural. " Some concrete stairs."

" And that was all? "

I frowned as if I didn't understand him. " I didn't actually see it happen," I said.

" No? Ah well, perhaps he'll be able to tell us more himself presently."

As I went back to the waiting-room, the bag over my arm seemed to weigh a ton. I had wanted to tell the doctor what I believed had really happened. I wanted to call the police and tell them too and to send them as vengefully as possible after the two men whom I had seen come out of the block of flats. But because of what I had found amongst Peter's vests and pants, I didn't dare say a word to anyone until I had spoken to him.

Sitting down on the same hard chair as before, I thought that Peter himself probably wouldn't remember much about the attack on him. He might never have seen the two men and only have gone down suddenly and incredibly into blackness. But he ought to remember how that jewellery had got into his drawer.

He had better remember, I thought. And he had better be honest with me about it. . . .

At that point, just as if someone had unexpectedly laid a hand on my shoulder, I went stiff on my little chair, and I know something strange showed on my face, because an anxious-looking, elderly man sitting opposite

me made a quick movement of concern and I think would
have got up and come to me if I hadn't reached out for
one of the dog-eared magazines on the table before me,
and started turning the pages. The pictures all swam
together and meant nothing to me, so one of them, a
glossy thing, all sea-green and pink, which I believe was
somebody's dream-kitchen, seemed as good a thing as
any to go on staring at while I looked at that other
picture in my mind, that pattern in the events of the
last few days which I had suddenly and appallingly
recognised.

Jess was at the centre of it. Jess in the garden, jumping
up at Peter. Only it wasn't Peter, it was Tom. And Jess
was welcoming him because he wasn't a terrifying
stranger, he was her good friend. Her friend whom she
had learnt to trust, as she had me, by meeting him with
Peter. . . .

So far it was merely as Owen had suggested. But there
was more to it.

For if Peter had known Tom for some time, but kept
this secret, wasn't this because, most certainly, they had
been up to no good together? Tom wasn't the only one
who was capable of climbing up the side of a house.
Peter, his twin, could also climb like a cat. And together
they would have made a formidable team. Tom could
have created alibis for Peter, as easily as Peter could for
Tom. It could have been Tom who was usually out in the
open, drawing attention to himself, but always able, in the
last resort, to prove that he couldn't have been on the spot,
while it was actually Peter who did the job.

For instance, it could have been Peter who robbed the
Loaders, knowing that they went out every Sunday
evening and perhaps also knowing, although he had
denied it to his mother, that on that particular evening
they were going to visit Dr. Lindsay first. Peter's
antagonistic attitude to Margaret, the way that he had

suddenly fled from her, could all have been part of an act to explain his disappearance. He had been gone for at least half an hour. Since he knew the house, and perhaps even the safe, that might have been enough time for him and Margaret's jewellery could have been in his pockets when we drove back to London that evening.

But in that case, why had the partnership between him and Tom been broken up? Why had Tom been brought out into the open, for me to meet, for Dr. Lindsay and the Loaders to hear about?

Well, that was simple, wasn't it? It was because the meeting in the White Horse ought never to have happened. I hadn't at that time been meant to meet Tom. Tom hadn't been supposed to go to the White Horse at all. But Tom had taken to drinking harder, and had been growing unreliable and whatever his reasons for it might have been, had shown himself there, and to me, of all people. Perhaps that explained the terror that I had seen in Sandra's eyes that day.

In the end too it explained her fear and hatred of Peter, her visit to Dr. Lindsay's house and her threats, after the murder. It explained the murder.

With sudden repulsion as if I had been reading all these evil things on the shiny pages of the magazine I was holding, I thrust it away and stood up. I had been getting into deep water and I couldn't go on by myself. I needed advice.

Going to the desk, I told the woman there that I was leaving and that if I was wanted, I could be reached at an address which was that of the Barfoots' house in Hendon. I gave her the Barfoots' telephone number. Then I went out and at the first telephone box I came to, rang up Mr. Barfoot and said that I was on my way to see him.

I went by taxi. Rather to my surprise, when I arrived, I found Mrs. Barfoot at the gate, peering along the street, anxiously waiting for me. Her calm face was full of perturbed sympathy. When I paid off the taxi and came to the gate, she took both my hands, gave them a squeeze, then, instead of returning at once to her gardening, led the way into the house and into her husband's room. Silently, as always, she sat down in a chair near the door and waited for me to explain myself to him.

I hadn't thought, on my way, of the fact that the Barfoots would of course have read the papers and so would know, before I arrived, that I had got myself mixed up in a murder. It was a relief now to realise that I could skip a good deal of the explaining that I had been rehearsing in my head in the taxi.

Mr. Barfoot had been working at his lathe when Mrs. Barfoot and I came in. The floor around him was covered in shavings and several had stuck to his pullover and trousers. There was an excited glitter in his eyes as he tried to get me settled at once in a chair and talking. But I told him that first I wanted to telephone the hospital where I had left my husband.

His eyebrows shot up in astonishment, but he had the sense to wave me to the telephone without demanding explanations first. When I got through to the hospital, I was told that Peter was resting comfortably, that his pulse rate and his temperature were still normal and that there was nothing for me to worry about.

Nothing, I thought. Nothing at all!

Mr. Barfoot had been snorting and fidgeting while he waited. As I put down the telephone, he burst out, "White beads, eh? And then a murder! Isn't it amazing? Well, in all seriousness, isn't it? I tell you, I've resisted superstition in others all my life—I've always considered it a duty—but there's nothing like having a good wallow in it oneself when occasion offers. And by Jove, hasn't the occasion offered! My dear Anne, ever since I read the papers this morning I've felt as if I'd somehow been endowed with the gift of prophecy. I practically told you something like this would happen— now didn't I? Lucy says of course I didn't, but how can she tell? She was out in the kitchen, cooking that fish-pie. I told you white beads were the very devil. And now there's the business of washing Simon in mafoi. Have you done that? It doesn't sound as if you had, or he wouldn't be in hospital. Well, perhaps he would—I don't want to lose my head about all this. Why is he in hospital, my dear? What's happened? "

I had been lighting a cigarette and took a long pull at it before I said carefully, " Who is Simon? "

" He means Peter, dear," Mrs. Barfoot said. " Daniel always gets names mixed up when he's excited and we've both been so terribly concerned for you both."

" And what's mafoi? " I asked.

" A concoction of leaves," Mr. Barfoot answered, " in which, if one twin dies, the surviving twin should be washed, to avert impending evil."

" More Upper Guinea? "

" Somewhere like that, I think," he said.

" Well, it's a little late to tell me about it," I said. " Two men waylaid Peter on our staircase this afternoon, banged him on the head and knocked him out—for all I know, they thought they'd killed him—and so he's in hospital."

" Good heavens! " Mr. Barfoot said. " Why, I never . . . I mean to say, I never imagined . . . Oh lord, please forgive my fooling, my dearest Anne! I hope the police have caught the thugs who did it."

" I don't think the police know anything about it yet, I said, " unless the doctor at the hospital told them. He was obviously suspicious."

He gave me a wondering look and said, " You mean you haven't told them yourself? "

" Not yet," I said.

"And I always thought you had a head on your shoulders."

"Well, I had a reason."

"So I should hope. It had better be a pretty good reason too, in the circumstances."

I opened my handbag, fished out the small handful of jewellery which had been lying at the bottom like a great lump of lead, held it out to him and let the pieces trickle into his hand. "Here it is," I said. "I found these amongst Peter's clothes in the flat just before we left for the hospital."

"Oh lord——" Mr. Barfoot looked in shocked dismay at what he was holding. "But that makes it worse, Anne—much worse!"

"Daniel," Mrs. Barfoot said warningly, "let Anne tell the story in her own way."

"Yes, yes," he muttered. "I'm sorry—I always talk too much. Anne knows it. Stop me next time, Anne. Now go ahead."

So I told him what had happened, beginning with Jess. I also told him about Geo. Biggs's van in the lay-by. But one always had to begin and end with Jess.

Settling down to be the good listener that he could be when he chose, Mr. Barfoot fiddled with the pieces of jewellery that I had given him, examining them one by one and laying them down on the edge of the table near him. Once he cocked a questioning eyebrow at his wife, to see if she wanted to examine them too, but she only gave a quick shudder and looked as if the mere thought of touching them made her want to hurry out again to her garden or her budgerigars.

At last, when I had finished, or almost finished my story and was telling of that pattern which I had perceived, as I sat in the waiting-room at the hospital, in the events of the last week or two, he suddenly swept all the pieces of jewellery up into his hands again.

"All right, there's no need to dot all the i's and cross the t's," he said. "You're afraid the boy's a thief—and if he's a thief, there's a quite good chance that he's a murderer too, though it doesn't necessarily follow——"

"Daniel!" Mrs. Barfoot cried. "She isn't afraid of anything of the sort." She turned to me. "Are you, dear?"

"Of course not," I said impatiently. "But that's what somebody wants me to think—or wants the police to think. And that's why I haven't been to them yet. *I* know Peter isn't a thief or a murderer, but my reasoning about that mightn't seem quite as good to them as it does to me, so I thought I'd like your advice first about what I ought to do. I don't want simply to walk straight into the trap that's been laid for us."

Mr. Barfoot tugged at his long chin.

"Reasoning, you say. You've done some reasoning, have you? Or is it just a case of loving and trusting?"

"Look, if you were a jewel-thief," I said, "and you didn't want your wife to know about it, would you hide any part of your loot in an unlocked drawer, amongst your underclothes? Wives have a way of washing things, and then putting them back where they belong. Peter knew I was certain to go to that drawer sooner or later. He'd never have been such a fool as to try to hide anything there."

"Dear, dear, how extraordinarily foolish I feel," Mr. Barfoot said. "I'm certainly slipping. All right then, the things were planted—clumsily planted—to make it look as if Peter was in with Tom. That's what you mean, isn't it? Now who do you think did that? Sandra?"

"I don't know," I said. "Not yet."

"I don't mean that Sandra did it herself," he said, "but suppose the two men who attacked Peter were friends of hers and Tom's, and suppose, when she rushed out of her mother's flat, she got hold of them and sent them off to your flat with these things and instructions to get in and hide them somewhere and then knock Peter out as soon as they got the chance. Then suppose one of them telephoned the police to tell them where the things were to be found."

"It doesn't sound an awfully clever scheme," I said.

"That's why I plumped for Sandra," he said. "She's made up her mind Peter killed Tom, hasn't she? And she thinks he's getting away with it and she's out for revenge—plain, not very subtle revenge. I think I'd rather like to meet Sandra, Anne. She seems to me much more important in all this than Jess. But you don't think so, do you? That poodle's at the centre of it for you."

I hesitated, then nodded. "I suppose I do."

"Let's consider this scatty animal, then," he said. "You assume that she'd go mainly by smell, and so could easily tell the twins apart, and so her behaviour in the garden, which you saw from Mr. Loader's car, is proof positive that it was Peter you saw then."

"Well, isn't it," I said, "unless she knew Tom already? "

"Let's suppose it's proof, anyway, for the moment. What does it mean? "

"That Peter couldn't have been picking Margaret Loader up at the bus stop when he said he was."

"And so is lying. Now why do you suppose he's lying? "

"Not because he's a murderer."

"All right. But he knows who is—is that what you think? "

I took a long time to answer, then said unwillingly, "Perhaps."

"Or thinks he knows," Mr. Barfoot said. "In any case, is lying for reasons connected with Margaret Loader."

This time I only met his look without trying to answer.

He nodded. "That's the trouble, isn't it? Were Peter and Mrs. Loader in that house for reasons nothing to do with murder or burglaries? Were they interrupted by Tom and did one of them shoot him? Or did Mrs. Loader go to the house with death for Peter in her heart and shoot Tom by mistake, and is Peter, for old time's sake or whatever, protecting her now by giving her that alibi? Or was there some connection between Mrs. Loader and Tom and did she know quite well whom she was shooting? She frequented the White Horse, didn't she? And it isn't unknown for a woman to arrange to have her own jewellery stolen, if it's well insured. But that still means that Peter's protecting Margaret Loader. Whatever way you look at it, that seems to be the answer, if it was Peter in the garden."

"Daniel, I don't think you're being very nice," Mrs. Barfoot said.

"Dear Lucy," he said, "I don't think Anne came here for me to be nice. Let's proceed. Suppose it wasn't Peter in the garden. Does that make things any better?"

"But you've got to explain why Jess was so glad to see him," I said.

"Of course. And the only explanations that anyone has thought of so far are that Tom knew her already, because he knew Peter, or else that he'd been making up to Jess in secret, so that she shouldn't upset his burgling the house, or else that the dog you saw wasn't Jess at all, but another poodle that looked just like her."

I nodded.

"And you've told me your objection to the first theory and there's the same objection to both the others—that our busy and successful burglar was taking an awful lot of trouble over a very unimportant piece of business."

"Yes."

"Well, I'm not sure if that's a sound objection," Mr. Barfoot said. "Tom may have been a perfectionist.

He may have taken as much trouble about a little haul as a big one."

"Yes, but why burgle Dr. Lindsay's house at all?"

"Just what I was going to say. But he did, or at least he went there. And if it wasn't to burgle the house, then it could only be to meet somebody. And who would that be but Peter? So we're back to Peter probably being on the spot, whichever way you approach the matter."

I am not sure why, but I had hoped that Mr. Barfoot would somehow be able to find a different answer for me. I had come to him for help and comfort and he wasn't giving me any. He had only said what I knew already and said it so baldly that there was nothing for me now but to face the truth and try to make up my mind what I felt about it.

Well, what did I feel? Mainly dread, I found, that Owen Loader, the other person who knew what I did, would sooner or later give his information to the police. If he did, of course, I could contradict him. I had already deceived the police by not telling them the whole of what I knew, so it wouldn't be difficult to go a little further and say flatly that neither Peter nor Jess had been in the garden when we passed in the car and that Owen was making up the story out of jealousy.

And that was what I would probably do. It was about all that I could do for Peter now. What happened afterwards, what I was going to feel when it was all over, was something that I needn't think about yet, though it seemed to me that the world would probably feel a very desolate place, without much hope in it.

Mr. Barfoot was continuing, "However, there are a few things I'd like to know more about. One's that girl Sandra. The other is that telephone call which her mother, apparently, didn't make. Who did make it and did Peter know all the time who it was, or was he taken

in? And there's another thing . . ." He paused for so
long that I looked up at him again. He was frowning
into the distance, his long nose twitching, as if he were
scenting something strange. " There's something . . .
Damn my memory! There's something I've heard sometime, but what it is . . ? "

" Something I've told you? " I asked.

" I don't know. It's important, I'm sure. Well, if it
is, it'll probably come back to me presently. Meanwhile,
we've got to decide what to do with these pretty things
you brought along with you." He opened the hand in
which he had been holding the jewellery. " I think I'm
going to take them along to a certain friend of mine at
Scotland Yard. Did you know I've a friend at Scotland
Yard—Superintendent Gee? I've all sorts of queer friends
in queer places. I think he can probably give me some
useful advice—yes? " He looked up inquiringly, because
I had jumped to my feet.

" Mr. Barfoot, if you go and tell a policeman one single
word of what I've told you——! "

He grabbed my hand and pulled me towards him.
" Now, now, trust me, Anne," he said. " Not a word
about Jess, naturally. But you don't want these things
on your hands any longer than you can help. You and
Lucy settle down and have a nice evening together, and
leave all this to me." He turned to his wife. " Isn't that
best, Lucy? Don't you agree? "

She gave him a brooding look and said, " I suppose so,
Daniel. But I think you should be very careful that you
don't talk too much to your friend at Scotland Yard or
anyone else. You know what you are."

" Of course I know and that's why I won't," he said
cheerfully and, patting my cheek, stood up, dropped the
jewellery into his pocket and, becoming suddenly very
jaunty, looking more than ever like my old rocking-horse,
recklessly going nowhere, started for the door.

"Wait a minute," I said. "If you're going, I'll go too."

"No," he said. "I want a very confidential talk with Gee."

"I didn't mean to Scotland Yard—I want to go back to the hospital," I said.

This was not the truth. But I thought that if I told the Barfoots where I was thinking of going they might make difficulties about it. As it was, Mrs. Barfoot only insisted that I should return to Hendon for the night, because a flat which had already been broken into once that day might not feel a pleasant place to spend a night in alone. I had been thinking this myself, so I promised willingly. We went out together, folded ourselves away inside the bubble-car and drove off.

As we drove through Golders Green and down the Finchley Road, Mr. Barfoot was silent, except that he muttered to himself occasionally in a resentful undertone. At Baker Street Station I asked to be let out, saying that I would take a taxi the rest of the way. Absently Mr. Barfoot stopped the car and I got out and went towards the mews where Ivy May lived.

I meant, if I found Sandra, to try to persuade her to go out to Hendon with me. If she wasn't there, I was going to try to find Ivy May's friend, Mrs. Barry, who had spent Saturday morning ironing her dresses in Ivy's flat and had sworn that Ivy couldn't have got to a telephone. If I couldn't find Mrs. Barry, I was going to start plaguing Ivy's other neighbours, to see if there was any small fact to be picked up which would make the number of Peter's lies to me seem fewer and more understandable. If that didn't work, I should at least have got through the evening, have worn myself out and become ready to go back to Hendon to face the night ahead. Going up to the lilac-coloured door, I rang the bell.

At once footsteps clattered down the stairs inside and

the door was thrown open. Sandra stood there. Seeing me, she gave a queer little moan, grasped one of my arms, dragged me in and slammed the door. Then she let go of me and sagged against the wall, as if she had barely the strength to stand.

"How is he—go on, go on, tell me!" she said. "Was he hurt bad? Is he all right? . . . Oh God, I tell you, Anne, if I'd known, I'd never have done it, never! I swear I wouldn't've!"

She started to cry, noisily, like a child, in mingled despair and terror.

"If I'd known, I'd never have harmed him," she sobbed out again. "It was just believing it was him did it to Tom. . . ."

"Known *what*?" I shouted at her.

"That Mum did make that call in the morning, of course," she said. "I don't know why. I don't understand. But she did it—she double-crossed Tom and me." She pushed herself away from the wall and made an effort to steady her voice. "For all I know, she shot Tom herself. Come upstairs—I'll tell you."

CHAPTER XIII

I FOLLOWED HER up the steep little staircase into Ivy May's sitting-room. It smelt of stale beer and soot. The number of bottles on the hearth and of shoes, stockings and newspapers strewn about the floor had grown. In the twilight the room looked incredibly forlorn and dingy.

Sandra switched on a light in one of the wobbly table lamps and drew the curtains.

"Mum's out at her job," she said, handing me a sheet

of paper which had been lying on the mantelpiece. " This
is what she left me."

There were a few lines written in pencil in a huge
scrawl on the sheet of paper.

" Not to worry, I'll be back at the usual time, look
after yourself, love."

I handed the note back to Sandra. " Is that all? She
doesn't say anything about that telephone call."

Sandra's thin fingers with the long sharp nails at the
ends of them, crumpled up the piece of paper and hurled
it down amongst the beer bottles.

" Of course she doesn't."

" Then how d'you know about it? "

" Never mind how I know."

" I do mind," I said. " I want to know all about it.
How do you know she made that call? "

Sandra drew a sharp little breath of exasperation, as
if she found my mind intolerably slow.

" Because Edna brought the change round," she said.
" Edna's a fool. She told me all I needed to know before
she knew she'd said anything at all. ' Here's her change,'
she said, ' and tell her that head-scarf wasn't a present,
I want it back,' she said."

Sandra threw herself down into one of the little arm-
chairs. She seemed to think that that had made everything clear to me.

" Who's Edna? " I asked.

" Edna Barry."

" Oh, the Mrs. Barry who spent the morning here,
doing her ironing."

She gave a contemptuous laugh. " And said Mum
never went out. You can tell what happened, can't you?
They're great friends, her and Mum. Mum's always
using her phone. So when Mum wants to phone yesterday
without letting anyone know, she goes and fixes up for
Edna to come and do her ironing here and swear Mum

never went out. Then Mum borrows her coat and
head-scarf and glasses—Edna wears those kind of jewelled
glasses that go up at the corners and make your face all
different—and Mum pops along to Edna's and does her
phoning and comes back in a minute or two with one of
Edna's dresses over her arm, so if anyone sees her they'll
think it's Edna fetching something more to iron. And
Mum gives Edna ten bob to pay for the call and Edna
hasn't got the change, so she brings it back to-day.
Well, there you are."

I had pushed some newspapers off a chair and sat down.

" If Edna really did something like that for your
mother," I said, " wouldn't she at least expect to keep the
change? "

" Not with all the things Mum's got on her. They're
friends, I tell you. Only they've no brains, neither of
them. Mum goes and forgets to give Edna back her
head-scarf and Edna goes and gives me the change for the
ten bob and says she wants her scarf back—*me!* She says
that to *me!* " Sandra started to cry again, her words
fading into a thin little screech above the sobs. " Mum
never liked Tom. She never wanted me to take up with
him. I used to think it was jealousy, because she knew
him first and thought he was after her, when it was
always me he wanted. But I never thought she'd go and
help his murderer! And the way she lied to me, pretending
she was sorry . . . ! " A string of foul words poured out
between Sandra's swollen lips until her own sobs choked
her.

" So she was helping his murderer, was she, by getting
Peter and me out of the way? " I said. " She wasn't
merely clearing the scene for Tom to do his job? "

Sandra sat upright in her chair. Gulping back her
tears, she said violently, " Listen, she knew Tom was
going to do that himself. She knew it. She knew he was
going to phone you and Pete and get you to go into

Lachester to meet him, just like he did. That would have got Pete out of the way without getting him into any trouble. Tom sort of took a liking to Pete, he didn't want to get him into trouble. And he told you to tell him—I know he did, I was there beside him—he told you to tell Pete to keep clear of us in future. Didn't he? "

" Yes," I admitted. " He did."

" That was to keep Pete out of trouble. But Mum went and phoned Pete first and got him to go and meet her at a place that didn't exist on purpose to get Pete *into* trouble, on purpose so she could say she never phoned him and make it look as if he was lying about everything."

" Only suppose I'd gone with him," I said. " I nearly did—only we had a quarrel that morning."

" That wouldn't have helped him much. A wife's word never helps a fellow much." It sounded as if she spoke from bitter experience. " Besides, maybe Mum knew he'd manage it so you didn't go with him."

" I don't understand," I said.

She gave me a swift, sly look, then looked down at the floor again.

" Well, never mind," she said. " That's his business."

I got up and stood over her. " What do you mean, Sandra? "

" Oh, be your age," she said.

In a voice that surprised me, it was so quiet and deadly, I said, " Sandra, you told me it was you who arranged that attack on Peter, and you know he could easily have been killed. Do you realise it's going to be quite simple to bring that home to you, because I saw your two friends leaving after they'd done it—done that and planted the jewellery in our flat. Yes, I know about that too. So you'd better tell me what you mean. And you'd better tell me something else, and that's who murdered Tom. Because you know who it was, don't you? "

Her bony body went slack in the chair. In an odd, listless tone, she answered, " I told you I'd never have done any of it, Anne, if I'd known about Mum and that phone call. It was only me thinking—it was them making me think—it was Pete shot Tom and was getting away with it too. I'm sorry, Anne, truly I am."

" That's easy to say," I said.

" It's the truth. I'd never have wished Pete any harm except for that."

" Well, go on and tell me the rest," I said. " Who was your mother helping when she made that call to Peter? Who told her to do it? "

" That's my business now," Sandra said in the same listless tone, which I found far more disturbing than her violence, for the violence came and went in a moment, but behind the listlessness there was the dreary acceptance of a desperate purpose in life.

I went on urgently, " Don't keep saying that, Sandra. You can't do anything by yourself, or even with those friends of yours. About the only thing you can do for Tom now is tell the police what you know about the murder."

" And then what? " she asked. " Sit around waiting to get murdered too? "

" They'd take care of you."

But I saw that I was going to get nowhere at all with that line of argument. Whatever her other fears and suspicions, the police remained the worst enemy of all. So I tried to persuade her to go with me to Hendon to talk to Mr. Barfoot.

I did it without much hope of success and was surprised, first at her wary questions about who he was and why she should talk to him, and then still more when she said abruptly that she didn't mind, she'd go to see him if I liked. Standing up, she looked round for her waterproof and seemed in a hurry to be gone. It was, of course,

extremely naïve of me to believe that she meant it.
Outside in the mews she walked along beside me rather
slowly until we reached the street, then she began to
hurry and just before we reached Baker Street, she jumped
into a taxi, slammed the door in my face, shouted out
something to the driver and got away from me.

Disconcerted and muddled, I stood still, looking after
the taxi without any thought of trying to follow it.
Even if another taxi had passed just then, I don't think
I should have had the courage to leap into it, crying,
" Follow that cab! " After a minute I walked on to the
nearest bus stop, got on to the next bus to Golders Green,
presently changed buses there and so returned to the
Barfoots.

Mr. Barfoot had not come home yet, but supper was
ready in the kitchen and Mrs. Barfoot insisted that I sit
down to it straight away. Except that I first telephoned
the hospital again, to be told, as before, that Peter was
resting comfortably, I did as she wanted and discovered a
ravenous hunger. I ate two chops and a lot of mashed
potatoes and french beans, some bread-and-butter
pudding and some cheese and biscuits. A secret sort of
glee appeared on Mrs. Barfoot's face as she watched me.
She said she had thought that I would probably need
something substantial, but that it would be much easier
to make Daniel eat his nice piece of steamed fish if he
hadn't got to watch me eating grilled chops.

He came in when we were drinking tea in the sitting-
room.

Saying that she would put his supper on a tray, so that
he could sit with us, Mrs. Barfoot went out to the kitchen
and Mr. Barfoot dropped wearily into a chair, gently
rubbed his stomach, as if it needed comforting, groaned,
shut his eyes and for a moment, resting silently, looked
old, fragile and helpless. Then he opened his eyes again
and their bold glare brought the life back into his face.

Groping in one of his pockets, he brought out the jewellery which I had seen him stow there before he started out.

"But I thought you were going to turn that in to your friend at Scotland Yard!" I exclaimed.

"Mm—yes—changed my mind, however," he said.

"Why?" I asked, wondering if by any chance it was possible that he had simply forgotten what he had started out to do.

"Thought of something more important," he said, but he was looking puzzled about the jewellery, as if really he could not quite remember how it had come to be in his possession. Putting it down on the arm of his chair, he went on, "Well, it seemed to me it was more important, but now I've still got these damned things to dispose of, haven't I? I wonder if a nice little hole in the garden wouldn't really be the best place for them. Least said, soonest mended—and I'm sure no one would ever suspect Lucy of having stolen gems hidden under her sweet peas."

"What did you think of that was so important?" I asked.

"Oh yes—well, it's complicated," he said. "I had an idea. It seemed to me I remembered something. Something about twins, you know. I'd read it somewhere. . . .'

"Mr. Barfoot!" I said fiercely. "You haven't been spending your time reading about white beads, or iguana lizards, or twins turning into monkeys or anything like that! Not this evening, with those things in your pocket!"

"Now, don't get excited," he said. "I told you it was complicated. No, I haven't been reading anything. What I said is, I *remembered* reading something. I thought about it all the way in to Baker Street, where I put you down, but I couldn't recall just how it went, or where I'd read it, or whom it was by. That's the worst of being the omnivorous, disorganised sort of reader I am. I've got too many facts in my head without the connecting links you need to make sense of them. But I thought of somebody who ought to be able to put me on the right road, if I could get hold of him. So that's what I did instead of going to Scotland Yard. I went looking for this man. I'd have telephoned him, only I couldn't remember his name. That's because I'm worried. I never can remember names when I'm worried. Actually it turned out to be Shurmer—Walter Shurmer. Dr. Walter Shurmer, F.R.S. It all came back as soon as I got to his house. I went there once to some meeting or other in the days when I still had to go to meetings. It's in South Kensington. And very fortunately he was at home this evening and was very kind and helpful. He said he thought he knew what I was talking about——"

" A very clever man! " I said.

" Oh yes," Mr. Barfoot said, " I admire him without reservation too, so let's have less of the sarcasm. But unluckily he hadn't got the book himself and on a Sunday evening, of course, I couldn't get it anywhere else. Never mind, I'll get it first thing to-morrow. He wrote the name down for me and I'll go out first thing in the morning and we'll have everything cleared up in no time. . . ." He stopped to give a great yawn and his head fell back on the cushions behind him. " Go to bed early to-night, get up early to-morrow, clear everything up in no time," he muttered, his eyes closing.

If Mrs. Barfoot had not come in then with his supper, he would have gone straight to sleep.

A grim sense of disappointment kept me practically silent for the next twenty minutes or so, while Mr. Barfoot pecked disconsolately at his steamed fillet of lemon sole, then went on to a small baked custard. I don't know what I had expected of his trip to Scotland Yard, but certainly not that he would simply not go there at all, but go chasing after some more of the pointless sort of information about twins which he seemed to love, arriving home too tired even to tell me about it.

And it was getting late to tell the police the truth about the attack on Peter and my discovery of the jewellery in his drawer. For by now Peter himself might have been doing some talking and whatever he had chosen to say, I didn't want to run the risk of contradicting it until I had had the chance of some discussion with him.

I sat there fretting and glowering until Mr. Barfoot, a little revived by food, remarked, " I could tell you the rest of it, I suppose, but I'd sooner wait till I've looked it up. I could be wrong, and then you'd only feel more mixed up than ever. Yes, I think I'll wait. But now tell me what you've been doing with yourself. And how's Peter? "

" Resting comfortably, whatever that means," I said.

" It means he's got a splitting headache, feels sick, wishes he was dead, is afraid he soon will be, but isn't actually in danger—cheer up! " Mr. Barfoot said.

" As a matter of fact, I didn't go back to the hospital when I left you," I said. " I went to see Sandra. I thought I'd try to bring her to see you, but it didn't work. She agreed, just as a way of getting rid of me, then vanished in a taxi. I'd suggested she should tell the police what she knew—that was probably the trouble. But she did tell me something first. She told me her mother did make that telephone call to Peter."

Mr. Barfoot yawned and said he couldn't quite remember how the telephone call came in, so I reminded him of it, then told him what Sandra had told me about Mrs. Barry. He tried to listen, but his head began to nod and his eyelids to droop and I noticed that Mrs. Barfoot was anxiously watching the cigarette in his hand, in case he should let it slip out of his fingers and burn a hole in the carpet. Only when I told him about the end of my interview with Sandra, he opened one eye and looked at me fixedly with it.

" So she knows who did the murder, or thinks she knows," he said. " Poor girl, poor girl! What a pity you didn't manage to bring her here."

" I don't think you'd have managed to get anything out of her," I said. " She's grown up in the school that doesn't talk."

" I wasn't thinking of that," he said. " I was thinking of the fact that if she really does know anything, she's in danger. And so is the murderer, of course, from Sandra."

Mr. Barfoot stubbed out his cigarette, put his hands on his knees and got creakily to his feet. " Now I think it would be a good idea if we all went to bed," he said. " That's what I'm going to do, at any rate. I want to be up good and early, looking for that book Shurmer told me about."

Mrs. Barfoot at once began to put away her knitting, but I stayed where I was.

" If Sandra's in serious danger, isn't there anything we can do about it? " I asked.

" What, to-night? " he said. " Certainly not. We're all going to bed to get a good night's rest."

" But Mr. Barfoot——"

" Not to-night! " But he seemed to think that that must have sounded callous, for he added, " Anyway, what could we do, do you suppose? "

" Well, there's that friend of yours at Scotland Yard, whom you forgot to go and see. Couldn't he do something? "

" He probably knocked off work hours ago," Mr. Barfoot said. " Wait till the morning, when we'll all be more clear-headed. It's much too late now to do any more rushing around."

Mrs. Barfoot supported him and since for the two of

them it really was very late, I dropped the argument and went up to bed.

But it was not late for me and I expected to lie awake for an hour or two at least, my mind still helplessly plagued by the problems of the day. There was still that fearful problem, for instance, of what Peter had been doing when Owen and I had seen him in the garden with Jess.

What I really believed at that point must have happened was that Peter had picked Margaret up, as they had both said, at the bus stop near the White Horse, but that then, instead of going on to look for the café on the London road, they had returned to the Loaders' house and on the way had had some sort of emotional scene which had resulted, when they reached the house, in Peter's walking out in a hurry, as I knew he tended to whenever such a scene got going. He had returned to Dr. Lindsay's house, missing me at the bus stop near it by only a moment. Margaret had followed him and in crazy rage had tried to shoot him. Instead, she had shot Tom. Then the rage had passed and remorse and terror been left behind and she had clung like a child to Peter, whom she had wanted to kill, and he had promised to protect her. . . .

I went on thinking round and round this explanation of things until exhaustion suddenly washed over me in a great dark wave and I was half-asleep already when I reached out to turn off the light. So the sound of Daniel's bubble-car starting up in the road didn't seem surprising because it could only be part of a dream.

CHAPTER XIV

IN THE MORNING I found that it hadn't been a dream. Mr. Barfoot's insistence that nothing could be done about the danger to Sandra until next day had been a stratagem to get me to bed. Mrs. Barfoot told me that they had both felt sure that that was the best thing for me. But as soon as they had been sure, from the sound of my movements overhead, that I was in bed, Mr. Barfoot had set out to see if he could find Superintendent Gee.

Returning home very late, he had gone out again very early this morning, without telling his wife what he intended to do or when he was likely to return.

She did not appear worried by this. She foresaw a nice peaceful day ahead, all alone with her budgerigars. Her husband's movements had always been uncertain, largely because he changed his mind so often, and to have let herself worry about him would have been to let herself become a nervous wreck years ago. And it wouldn't have been at all sensible, Mrs. Barfoot thought, to have let herself become a nervous wreck, perhaps with an ulcer too, for what on earth would they have done if there had been two of them?

" And now, dear, I suppose you'll be going to the office again," she said as we finished breakfast. There was hopefulness in her tone at the thought of how nice it would be to have the house all to herself. " It's been very nice to have you and you must come again with Peter as soon as he's better. And you must take care of yourself too. Daniel said I should tell you most particularly to take care of yourself, if you insisted on going out. I think he was thinking that some bad characters might be thinking perhaps that poor child Sandra told you what she knows. But I don't think you should worry too much about that. Take sensible precautions, of course, but never worry more than you can help. What will be, will be."

I think she meant this to be cheering. When I left, she limped out to the gate with me, kissed me and stood watching me as I went off down the road. I have never doubted that Mrs. Barfoot was sincerely fond of me, but at the same time that she was always very happy to see the last of me, or of anyone else who invaded her contented solitude.

I didn't go to the office. I telephoned instead, to beg the day off, then I went to the hospital.

There they told me that Peter had left late the night before. They had advised against it, they said, and now refused to take any responsibility. A curt, irritable woman behind a desk washed her hands of him. I suppose she wasn't to be blamed, but I got curt and irritable too and asked if no one had troubled to give him the address and the telephone number of the friends with whom I had stayed the night and if they hadn't, what were things coming to? She said she didn't know if anyone had given him the message, she hadn't been on duty, and she personally thought that things were coming to a pretty pass.

Going out into the street again, all of a sudden I felt wildly frightened.

From the nearest telephone box I rang the number of our flat. There was no answer. But in case Peter had been there and had left some message, I decided to go back to it. He would have had to go to Belsize Park if he had wanted the car, and in any case, if he hadn't been given my message, the flat was the place to which he was most likely to have gone. And I found, when I reached it, that in fact he had slept the night there and had left a message for me, propped against the kettle in the kitchen.

The message said, " If you come back—have gone to Lachester."

It didn't say anything about how long ago he had left, or what he expected me to do, or how he was. And there was something about those first four words that set some nerve in me quivering. Where did he imagine I had been? What did he think I had been doing? With resentment mixing itself into my anxiety, I realised that I had better go to Lachester too. First, however, I telephoned Dr. Lindsay's house, but when Mrs. Joy answered she told me that there was no one but herself at home. Dr. Lindsay was out on her rounds and they hadn't seen or heard anything of Mr. Peter that day.

I asked Mrs. Joy to tell whichever of them she saw next that I was on my way down, then I set off for Lachester by Green Line bus.

That gave me about two and a half hours of sitting still, wondering about what was ahead of Peter and me.

The day was one of those clear, quiet summer days that feel so still, so calm, so settled that they seem to promise days and days to come of the same sunshine and deep, cloudless skies. It was the kind of day on which it feels mildly criminal to do anything but lie in the sun and dream, a feeling which makes pain and worry, if they can't be shed, cast an even harsher shadow than usual. I began to feel clammy and hot in the bus, wondering restlessly where and how Peter and I would take up the thread of our life together again, that thread which was almost too short to grasp, while its strength was being so violently tested. Part of me had no confidence in it at all and even believed that it had really snapped already. Yet that part of me didn't seem entirely real. It seemed to be outside of me, looking at me with a wary, warning eye, while the rest of me clung to the conviction that, for reasons I couldn't possibly have explained, Peter and I were immune to disaster.

The bus seemed to be travelling unbearably slowly and the light in my eyes was uncomfortably bright. Then as we approached Lachester, the bus seemed to go too fast, so that I longed for it to slow down, to give me more time for my unproductive brooding. Then all of a sudden I was on my feet, stumbling along to the door and asking the conductor to put me down.

He rang his bell and the bus stopped a little way beyond the roundabout near the White Horse. Getting out, I started walking back towards the pub. Before I had gone half-way I was convinced that I was a fool and that I couldn't have seen what I thought I had as we passed, which was Daniel Barfoot walking in at the door. However, as there wasn't likely to be another bus for some time and as there could be no harm in making sure, I went on and in the car-park of the pub, next to Geo. Biggs's van, I found the bubble-car, and a moment later, in the bar, Mr. Barfoot himself, ordering himself a whisky.

I didn't like to think what Mrs. Barfoot would have said, if she had known of this, for he was not allowed spirits of any kind, but at the same time I noticed something which I found almost as shocking. Mr. Biggs was in his usual corner, but instead of the double whisky which seemed to fit naturally into the curve of his hand, he was holding a glass of tomato juice.

He was looking no better for the change. His shifty little eyes, peering out from under the brim of his hat, looked bleary and anxious. There was an air of embarrassment about him, almost of shame. His leathery face looked yellower than I remembered it. He saw me, but revealed that he recognised me only by blinking his eyes several times, then staring down fixedly into his drink.

I went up to Mr. Barfoot and said, " Don't you think you might have told me you were going to do this? You could have saved me my bus fare."

He started and said, " How I hate being crept up on
from behind! My dear, when I left this morning, you
were so soundly asleep it would have taken a Chinese
brass band to waken you. I've been told Chinese brass
bands are the noisiest things there are. Yet they like to
have them at funerals and one of their favourite tunes is
' Auld Lang Syne.' Sufficiently appropriate, I suppose.
Well, since you're here now, what would you like to
drink? "

As I answered that I didn't want anything, but would
like Mr. Barfoot to drive me on to Lachester, Mr. Galpin
the landlord, moving towards us, said, " Good morning,
Mrs. Lindsay. We haven't seen you and your husband
here since that shocking business of Saturday, have we?
I must say, I felt very bad when I heard about it. I
thought of your meeting here and so on—and my handing
on that note you left behind. Not that any of us could
have told what it would lead to. . . . Yes, George? "

Mr. Biggs had just slammed his glass down on the
counter.

" The same," he said, barely audibly.

" The same—are you sure, George? " Mr. Galpin asked
with raised eyebrows.

" Isn't that what I said? " Mr. Biggs demanded.

" You wouldn't like some vodka in it? "

Mr. Biggs looked as if the suggestion made him want
to vomit. Mr. Galpin gave a shrug of his heavy shoulders
and filled the glass up with tomato juice, adding Worcester
sauce and a squeeze of lemon juice.

" I hardly like to take your money for it, George," he
said as he pushed it back to Mr. Biggs.

" You never like to take my money! " Mr. Biggs said
sullenly. " What's wrong with my money, eh? Tell me
that, Mr. Bloody Galpin, what's wrong with my money? "

A small man, standing near Mr. Biggs, patted him on
the arm and said quickly, " Here, take it easy, George.

Remember you aren't yourself. Mr. Galpin was only joking."

"That's right, George," Mr. Galpin said. "Sorry—no offence."

"I don't like your jokes," Mr. Biggs said.

"Take it easy, take it easy," the little man said fussily. Turning to Mr. Barfoot and me, he went on, "George hasn't been himself since Saturday. He took a turn, Saturday. Went out like a light when he was in his van. Nasty experience. Luckily for him, I came by, saw how it was, drove him home before the police could get him for being drunk-in-charge. Not that he was drunk—I've never seen George what you'd call drunk—but he took a turn."

"All right, all right, I said thank you, didn't I?" Mr. Biggs went on as angrily as ever. "D'you have to tell everyone about it? You've done nothing but talk about it ever since. What d'you want me to do, get down and lick your boots for saving my life?"

"Not your life, your driving-licence, George," the small man answered. "And you needn't go on trying to insult me, because I'm making allowances for you, see? You had a shock and I'm a man who understands shocks, so there you are."

Mr. Biggs looked as if he didn't like being understood any more than he liked his tomato juice.

Mr. Barfoot looked vaguely from him to Mr. Galpin and then back to the small man. "Saturday? A shock?" he said. "Not connected, surely. . . ."

"Ah, but that's just what it was!" the small man said excitedly. "And that's why it was such luck for George, me coming by. A bit later the place would have been swarming with police. They couldn't have helped but take him in. But I came along on my bike and saw his van in the lay-by and George flopping over the wheel, dead to the world and when I tried to wake him I couldn't get a sign of life out of him, so I pushed him over to the side, put my bike on board and drove him home and where the shock came in was when he found out how near he'd been to that horrible murder. Right on the spot, practically, not two minutes away! If the police had found him there, it'd have been the end of George, that's what it would've been."

Mr. Biggs brought the flat of his hand down on the bar with a sound like a shot.

"If I hear that once more there's going to be another horrible murder in Lachester!" he shouted.

"That's all right, George," the small man said. "I'm making allowances."

"I heard nothing, I seen nothing, I know nothing!" Mr. Biggs roared. "What are you trying to do to me? Make out I was mixed up in it? Make out I knew what our Albert was up to when he came here?"

"Calm down, George," Mr. Galpin said sharply. "We don't want that sort of talk here." He turned to Mr. Barfoot and me with a look of apology. "Actually I suppose it was pretty upsetting. He'd taken a queer sort of liking to that young man who was killed. Anyway, he's been off his liquor ever since, which is something I never thought I'd live to see."

"I tell you what, Mr. Galpin," Mr. Biggs said, leaning heavily on the bar and thrusting his head forward towards the landlord, "I don't like the way you talk any more than you like the way I talk. I don't like the way you talk, or the way you look, or your tomato juice or your lousy pub or the kind of company you let come into your lousy pub. And you don't like my money, eh? I spend my money here just like anyone else and you don't like it. Well, that's all right with me, Mr. Galpin, because I'm not going to spend any more here, see?" He burst into a fit of frenzied laughter. "Good-bye, Mr. Galpin—. this is the last you'll see of me and my money!"

As he strode towards the door, Mrs. Galpin appeared at it. He stood still, making her an elaborate bow and waving her to enter with profound, ironic courtesy. She came in, looking flustered and bewildered.

" Whatever's happened to him? " she asked.

Her husband explained, " George has just threatened never to darken our doors again."

" My goodness, how I wish we could believe him," she said.

" We'll be poorer people, my love," Mr. Galpin said with a grin.

Mr. Barfoot grasped my elbow. " Come along, come along," he said in my ear. " We've got work to do."

He had just drunk his whisky at a gulp and it had brought a flush to his cheeks which I found disturbing. Nodding a hasty good-bye to the Galpins, he hurried me out. Mr. Biggs's van was just leaving the car-park. Mr. Barfoot hustled me into the bubble-car, pushed and pulled at various parts of it till it burst into noisy life, then drove off after the van, remaining, however, at a safe distance behind it, for it swayed from side to side of the road as if the driver was as drunk as usual. Mr. Barfoot, folded up small over the wheel of the bubble-car, muttered in shocked astonishment at Mr. Biggs's survival on this earth.

" His good but unappreciated friend in there certainly did him a very good turn when he took him home on Saturday," he said, " but I'm afraid the rest of the community hasn't any reason to thank him. . . . There, look at that! "

The van had just taken a corner on the wrong side of the road and in some miraculous way been avoided by a lorry coming round the corner in the opposite direction.

" It makes you believe that some people are under the special protection of Providence, doesn't it? " Mr.

Barfoot went on. " If I'd tried to do that, I'd be dead—
stone cold dead—and so would you."

" Why are we following him, anyway? " I asked.

" To continue that remarkably interesting conversation.
Actually, I've an appointment in the White Horse in about
a quarter of an hour, but I don't suppose it'll matter if
I'm a little late for it.

" An appointment? " I said. " With whom? "

" With your Peter, as a matter of fact. Oh yes——"
he went on as I exclaimed in surprise, " that's why I
came down. I tried the hospital this morning, found he'd
gone, tried your flat—no good—tried Dr. Lindsay's
house, found he'd just got there; said I badly want a
talk with him. But at the moment I think a talk with
Mr. Biggs is more important."

" Because you believe he saw something from his van? "
My heart had started pounding so that I could scarcely
breathe.

" Perhaps. Not necessarily. There's the question of
why he went to that spot at all. As I've understood you,
Dr. Lindsay's house and that lay-by are on the other side
of Lachester."

" Yes, they are."

" Then it might be by chance that he was there and then
again, it mightn't."

" But you do think he could have seen Peter and Jess?
Even if he did, he'd have thought it was Tom, wouldn't
he? "

" Oh, about that . . . Take a look behind you, under
my mackintosh," Mr. Barfoot said. " There's a book
somewhere there that will interest you—*Outline of
Human Genetics*, by L. S. Penrose. I got it this
morning. . . ." He braked swiftly, because the van in
front had just lurched to a stop outside some yard gates
on which the words, " Geo. Biggs, General Dealer," were
painted.

Talking angrily aloud to himself, Mr. Biggs got down from the van and went to open the gates. They were beside a one-story wooden shack with a roof of corrugated iron and one dirty window in its side in which a broken electric fire, a roll of rusty barbed wire and several rows of old shoes were displayed. The shack was in a street which must once have been part of the old village of Sandy Green, for most of the buildings in it were small, stone-built cottages, standing in flower-filled gardens, but the blank wall of a factory loomed up behind them and at the end of the street, in what was left of a paddock, a row of new shops was being built.

Watching Mr. Biggs as he climbed back into the van and drove it into the yard, I said, " You haven't told me what happened last night when you went to see your Scotland Yard friend."

" Oh, we had a long talk," Mr. Barfoot said.

" Did you give him the jewellery? "

" Yes, I did." He opened the door of the bubble-car and motioned me to get out. " He promised to get in touch with Inspector Belden about it. Not that Gee has anything to do with the case here, of course, but I suppose communication isn't actually impossible. . . ." He got out of the car beside me and we followed Mr. Biggs into the yard.

Mr. Biggs took no notice of us. Unlocking the door of the shack, he went in and let it slam behind him. Rather cautiously, Mr. Barfoot opened it again and we both went in. Mr. Biggs had sat down in an old, half-broken rocking-chair in the middle of his shop. Surrounded by a macabre collection of old stoves, coal scuttles, shovels, a rusted radiator or two, and pieces of bedstead, with dust and cobwebs making a mystery of the shapes of them all, he had shut his eyes and started to rock himself feverishly.

Mr. Barfoot cleared his throat loudly and Mr. Biggs

opened his eyes. Still rocking, he gave Mr. Barfoot a
furtive stare, then looked at me, remembering me,
connecting me with Peter and Tom.

"All right, I know why you're here," he said, nodding
his head in time to the rocking. "You want to know what
I saw. That's it. Well, I saw plenty, let me tell you. A
man like me sees a lot of things. Oh yes. You may not
believe me. A lot of people don't believe me. Ignorant
people, they think they know everything in heaven and
earth. For instance, if I say I saw my old friend Mr.
Justice Robinson—I knew him years ago in the Far East,
a very highly educated, very distinguished man—well, if
I say I saw him coming towards me and saying, 'Now,
George'—he always called me George, we were great
friends—'Now George, don't meddle in this business—
I know what you're like, George, you've got a great sense
of duty, but in this particular business, don't let it run
away with you, see. Don't meddle!' Well, how much of
that are you going to believe?"

Mr. Barfoot had propped himself against the edge of an
old gas-cooker without any burners. He folded his arms.

"I think I'm prepared to believe most of it, Mr. Biggs,"
he said. "I'm only surprised that your vision spoke so
lucidly and sensibly. So often they only give very
unconvincing information about quite unlikely emotions
felt for one by one's departed relations. But your friend,
being a judge, had a trained mind, and that may have
helped. However, we aren't really nearly so interested in
what you saw as in what you expected to see."

Mr. Biggs checked his rocking for an instant. His lips
moved silently, as if he were repeating to himself what
Mr. Barfoot had said.

"We're interested," Mr. Barfoot went on, "in why you
went to that lay-by."

"So am I, if it comes to that," Mr. Biggs said, rocking
again and gazing upwards at the cobwebbed ceiling.

"But I can't tell you, Mr. Whoever-you-are, because
I don't know myself."

"You can't remember?"

"Can't remember a thing. Only my friend Mr. Justice
Robinson coming towards me and . . ."

He stopped as the door of the shack opened once more
and Owen Loader came in.

Seeing him, I realised that I had heard his car arrive
and his footsteps in the yard, but I had been too intent
on what Mr. Biggs was saying to take any notice. I
thought Owen was put out now at finding Mr. Barfoot
and me here before him, for his smile was uneasy as he
closed the door behind him.

As I introduced him and Mr. Barfoot to one another,
Owen said, "I suppose we're here for the same reason,
aren't we, Anne? You're wondering if Biggs could see
from that lay-by into Dr. Lindsay's garden."

I felt the heat of an angry flush in my cheeks. "I
thought nobody saw anything in Dr. Lindsay's garden,
Owen," I said.

He made a fumbling gesture with one hand towards
me. His healthy face had the slack, shadowed look of
someone who has not been sleeping. "Oh, that isn't
exactly what I meant. I thought——"

He was interrupted decisively by Mr. Barfoot. "If
you don't mind, Mr. Loader, Mr. Biggs was just in the
middle of explaining to us something which is of much
greater interest than Dr. Lindsay's garden." He turned
back to Mr. Biggs. "You say, Mr. Biggs, you remember
nothing but your vision of your friend, the judge, and his
excellent advice. By that you mean, don't you, that
you've no memory even of driving your van to the lay-by,
let alone why you did it?"

Mr. Biggs nodded several times. "And that's what
I told the police, word for word, as you've said it. You're
an intelligent man, sir, if I may say so."

" What's the last thing you do remember, apart from seeing the judge? " Mr. Barfoot asked.

Owen stirred restlessly, caught my eye and looked away.

" It's getting into my van and starting it," Mr. Biggs said. " That I remember clearly. I stayed till closing-time, got in the van and started it. And the next thing I remember is waking up here with that little perisher, Joe Cogley, standing over me telling me what a good friend he was to me. And that's what he's gone on telling me ever since—and I'm not denying it, mind! I'm not one to fail in gratitude to a friend. But one day soon, if he sticks around too much, he's going to find himself turning into a very absent friend—very, very absent."

" And how d'you explain this black-out of yours, Mr. Biggs? " Mr. Barfoot asked.

Mr. Biggs gave a sigh. " Well, I suppose I've been overdoing things lately. Working too hard and all. I wasn't drunk, if that's what you're thinking. I couldn't have been—I only had my usual. I reckon I drove off and then sort of lost my memory from all the overstrain of my life. But being a careful driver by instinct, I somehow got into that lay-by just before I passed right out."

" Do you remember who else was in the bar at closing-time? Were there many people? "

" 'Far as I remember, there was only one," Mr. Biggs said. " There were plenty up to dinner-time, but then mostly they went home."

" And who was this one person? "

A malicious little smile lifted one corner of Mr. Biggs's mouth. He nodded towards Owen.

" That gentleman's wife," he said.

Owen took a step forward. A wave of dark red mottled his cheeks. One of his fists clenched. But then he thrust it into a pocket, turned on his heel and went out. A moment later we heard the grinding of gears and some cursing, then the car went off.

Mr. Biggs's smile spread repellently across his face and he rocked himself with a new, enthusiastic energy.

"That's right. She took a nice lot on board that morning, let me tell you," he said. "I was watching her. 'Lady,' I thought to myself, 'if that's how you're going on, you aren't going to be in any fit state to drive that nice car of yours.' But she hadn't got the car. When I went outside to get into the van, she was walking off down the road to the bus stop. And that's the very last thing I remember."

"Thank you," Mr. Barfoot said. "That's exceedingly helpful."

I wasn't sure that I understood what was helpful about it. I hadn't doubted that Margaret had been at the White Horse, or that Peter had picked her up at the bus stop near it, even if he had done so rather earlier than either had admitted. It was what they had done then that was really the question. But Mr. Barfoot was looking very pleased as he grasped my arm and drew me to the door. I thought that perhaps this was because, in this roundabout fashion, he had drawn from Mr. Biggs the information that he hadn't seen Peter and Jess in the garden. It felt wonderful to know that. Yet it seemed to me that Mr. Barfoot's expression suggested that he had achieved a good deal more than that.

As soon as we were in the yard I started to ask him what it was, but he hustled me back into the bubble-car and sent it bouncing on down the street towards the row of half-built shops at the end. Realising only then that this was a dead-end and that he had come in the wrong direction, he asked me in a pained way why I hadn't warned him when he started. I said that I hadn't known where he wanted to go and asked him again what had been so useful about what Mr. Biggs had told him.

He turned the car and he was level with Mr. Biggs's shop again before he answered, "Now be a good girl and give me a minute to think. There's a lot to think about in what he told us."

"Well, at least tell me where we're going now," I said.

"Back to the White Horse, of course, to keep my appointment with Andrew."

"Peter," I corrected him. "Perhaps he won't have waited."

"If he hasn't, we'll have to find him. ⁚ ⁚ . Hey!" Mr. Barfoot was peering into his mirror. "Anne, isn't that Geo. Biggs's van behind us?"

I turned my head. Following and rapidly overtaking us, was the small shabby van, swaying as erratically as usual and with Mr. Biggs bent over the wheel.

As it bore down on us and passed us, Mr. Barfoot said, "It looks as if he's found he can't live on tomato-juice and means to be at the White Horse before us. But how glad I am he tried that dim beverage just once in his life. If he hadn't, there'd have been no occasion for his little friend Cogley to speak to us and I might not have troubled to see any more of our Mr. Biggs."

I made an impatient noise. He turned his head for a brief glance at me and went on, "I'm sorry, my dear. I'm not trying to be deliberately mystifying. It's just that the matter's rather complicated and I'm not very good at explaining myself and driving this car at the same time. But I assure you that what he told us may be enough to prevent a second murder. It *is* enough, unless our luck's out and it's happened already."

Accelerating, he stayed as close as he dared on the tail of the van and when Mr. Biggs swung it into the car-park of the White Horse, with the accustomed action of a man turning in at his own front-gate, Mr. Barfoot followed and pulled up beside him.

CHAPTER XV

THE AUSTIN SEVEN was also in the car-park, so I knew
that Peter had arrived to keep his appointment with Mr.
Barfoot and had waited. There were two or three other
cars there too and in the bar there were about half a
dozen people. But Peter wasn't among them. He was
on the terrace. Through the picture-window at which,
a week ago, I had seen Margaret Loader, I saw him
sitting on the bench where he and I had sat that day, had
eaten our chicken sandwiches and talked of Tom Hearn.
To-day Peter was eating sandwiches again and the sunshine was as bright as it had been then, but now it was
Margaret who was sitting beside him.

He saw me at the window and waved. I turned, meaning
to point him out to Mr. Barfoot, and only then realised
that he had not followed me into the bar. Mr. Biggs was
there, being reluctantly served by a tight-lipped Mrs.
Galpin, but of Mr. Barfoot there was no sign.

Going out again into the polish-scented hall, I saw
him in a telephone box at the foot of the stairs. Rapping
on the glass and pointing towards the door on to the
terrace to let him know where I was going, I left him
there, dropping in his pennies.

Peter stood up as I approached, but he did not come to
meet me. There was a dressing on his forehead and his
face was pale. It was remarkably blank too, with the
blankness which he used, as I knew, to cover anger. In
anyone else, it might have been an unwelcoming scowl.
Margaret, on the other hand, gave me one of her
brilliant, sad little smiles, caught me by the arm and drew
me down on the bench beside her.

" We've been waiting here for that friend of yours,

Mr. Barfoot," she said. " He only asked for Peter, but Peter thought it would be best if I came too, so he came and fetched me. Is Mr. Barfoot here with you? "

" He's telephoning," I said. " He'll be out in a minute."

Still standing, Peter asked abruptly, " What does he want, Anne? "

" I don't know," I said.

" When he rang up, he said he thought that if he could clear up a few points, he could help us, but it doesn't seem to have been important enough for him to be punctual," Peter said.

" Well, he's busy trying to prevent another murder, I believe." My voice wasn't quite steady, because Peter's attitude was beginning to make me lose my temper. " What did you mean, anyway, by clearing out of the hospital like that without any warning? "

" Oddly enough, I wanted to get home to you," Peter said. " What do you mean, another murder? "

" I don't know," I said. " I don't know of whom, or by whom, or how, or where, or when. But I know you'd no business to leave the hospital till they said you were fit to go."

" If I'd realised you couldn't be bothered to wait around for me, I wouldn't have, but I'll know another time," he said. " Where did you go? "

" I spent the night with the Barfoots. Of course, if I'd realised you'd do anything so stupid as to leave the hospital, I'd have waited, but——"

" Stop it, stop it—both of you! " Margaret cried. " Anne, I'm so glad you're here. I've been telling Peter, I've been getting frightened. That stupid business about Peter in the garden, when really we were together over here—Owen absolutely believes it, you know, and he's been threatening me with it—yes, really threatening. I'd never have dreamt he was capable of saying some of the things he has. He's always been so reasonable, so really understanding ... But now I can't get him to listen to me at all. So I'm hoping perhaps he'll listen to you——"

She stopped, because Owen himself had just appeared on the terrace.

At sight of him, Peter gave me a swift, suspicious look, then started to fumble for cigarettes in his pocket. Margaret went still and quiet. But before she lowered her eyelids, to look composedly at the paving-stones of the terrace, I caught a glimpse of the fierce emotion that I had once before surprised on her face.

Without looking up at Owen as he joined us, she asked softly, " What are you doing here, Owen? "

" Looking for you," he answered. His face still had the slack, blotched look of exhaustion that it had had in Mr. Biggs's shop.

" What made you think you'd find me here? " she asked.

He gave a brief glance at Peter, full of venom and pain.

" You've taken to coming here rather often lately, haven't you? " he said. " As a matter of fact, however, I came here partly because, like Anne and Mr. Barfoot, I was keeping an eye on George Biggs. We all met in Biggs's shop a little while ago and I didn't manage to have the conversation with him that I wanted."

" What do you want with Biggs? " Margaret asked.

" I want to find out what he saw from that van of his before he drove it into the lay-by on Saturday afternoon."

" So we're back to that, are we? " Peter said. " Jess and me in the garden. I tell you, Owen, if Biggs saw anyone, it was Tom."

Owen appeared not to have heard him. " Margaret, for God's sake, can't you trust me? " he said. " That's all I'm asking. I don't want to give you away, any more than Anne does."

She looked up at him suddenly.

" Give just what away, Owen? "

" I don't know! And that's what I can't stand—don't you realise? The only thing I know is that you and Peter are lying. And I'm afraid Biggs knows it too and sooner or later, when the police put pressure on him, he'll let out that he knows you were there."

She leant a little forward on the garden seat, her eyes steadily on Owen's now.

" But what was I doing there, Owen? You've looked accusations at me ever since Saturday, but you haven't told me what you believe I was doing."

" Didn't you at least see the murder? " he said. " Don't you know how it happened? "

She swayed in her seat, as if she were suddenly dizzy. " Oh God . . ." she muttered helplessly. " Why can't you believe me? Why have you and Anne made up this horrible thing about me? What are you trying to do to me? "

He said wearily, " If you'd only admit it, both of you, it would really make things much easier for Anne and me. Trying to lie for you, when we're in the dark, puts quite a strain on us. Almost more of a strain, I'm beginning to feel, than I can take."

Margaret turned quickly to me. " You see, Anne! He's threatening me—he is! And there's nothing I can tell him! "

" I'm not threatening, I'm warning you," Owen said. " I just want you to understand, I'm getting tired of lies—of yours and my own."

Peter's hand fell on Margaret's shoulder, steadying her.

" Do you realise, Owen, you're calling your wife a liar only because of some queer behaviour on the part of a poodle, which you imagine you saw? To me it appears that you're deliberately frightening her with this story about Jess. And what I'd like to know is, why are you doing it? Why has it suddenly become important to you to frighten Margaret? What are *you* afraid she might have seen over there? "

Owen flushed darkly. " I'm doing nothing of the sort," he said. " And there was no imagination in what I saw. Ask Anne if there was."

" A lot of imagination has gone into the construction you put on it," Peter said.

" Imagination! " Owen shouted. " I tell you, I've done everything I could to keep some hold on my imagination. And a lot of help I've had from you. You trust each other, but you don't trust Anne or me. You go on lying, and always together—as you were together at the time of the murder on Saturday, and as you're here together to-day. What are you doing here to-day— will you tell me that? "

" We came to meet Anne's friend, Mr. Barfoot," Peter answered quietly.

" *Why together?* "

Peter's brows twitched, as if the mere noise of it made his bruised head hurt.

" Because we'd realised your suspicions were becoming dangerous, Owen, and we wanted to talk it over. From something Mr. Barfoot said on the telephone, we thought he might be able to help us." He turned to me. " Isn't that so, Anne? "

Owen glanced at me. " She doesn't know," he said. " She might say it was, because you want it, but you can see from her face, she doesn't know any more about that than I do. The one thing she and I do know is that you were at home in the garden with Jess at a time when you and Margaret both swear—both of you!—that you were over here, looking for that café."

With relief, I saw that Mr. Barfoot had just reappeared on the terrace. Behind him came Mr. Galpin, carrying a tray of drinks. Owen had been talking so loudly that both of them had heard him. I saw Mr. Galpin pause for a moment, looking startled, but Mr. Barfoot came hurrying on, a book in his hand and a flustered frown on his face.

I started to introduce Peter and the Loaders to him, but he interrupted me impatiently, " Now, now, let's deal with that business of the dog and get it out of the way once and for all." Dropping on to a garden chair, he fluttered the pages of the book. " It's all a mistake and it's far better the police shouldn't hear anything about it. I've just telephoned for them, by the way. No—wait! " He wagged an authoritative finger as Owen started to speak again. " Listen to this, Mr. Loader. And you, Anne. It's from the *Outline of Human Genetics*, by L. S. Penrose, page ninety. ' Since identical twin pairs carry sets of the same genes, they have in common all characters which immediately result from one set of genetical instructions. Thus they have all their blood group antigens in common and also their basic biochemical peculiarities. Some chemical peculiarities are manifested in the composition of sweat, which varies slightly in different people but which is the same in identical twin pairs. Since dogs use the smell of sweat for identifying their masters, their friends and their enemies, they usually find it impossible to distinguish identical twins '."

He stopped and slammed the book shut. There was silence on the terrace. To me it seemed a long and deep silence in which nothing around us stirred, but yet in which a chill shadow seemed to melt away out of the sunlight.

" But then . . ." Owen said in a bewildered way. " But then . . . Were they speaking the truth all the time? "

" Were *they* speaking the truth? " Margaret asked with as much bewilderment. " They weren't making it up? "

She gave a shaky laugh and held out a hand to Owen. Neither Peter nor I spoke, but as we looked at one another, with Margaret sitting between us, I felt as if we had suddenly found ourselves alone together for the first time.

"And I thought . . ." Owen said. A shudder ran through him. "I didn't think it was only Peter. I was horribly afraid you were somehow in cahoots with that creature, Biggs, covering up for him when you knew he'd done the murder. I suppose he *is* the murderer? "

" But I didn't cover up for him," she said. " I saw him pass when I was waiting at the bus stop, but I didn't think it mattered. No one asked me anything about him."

" Yes, it was Anne and I who covered up for him—because we didn't believe you. I thought you were there in the house . . ." Owen's voice dried up again. He turned to Peter. " I wonder if there's any chance you're going to forgive me, either of you? "

Paying Mr. Galpin for the drinks that he had brought out to us, Mr. Barfoot said, " It seems to me a very natural mistake to have made in the circumstances. It's all too easy to make mistakes. About this man Biggs, for instance. If you'd told the police about his presence on the spot, they might have had the whole thing sorted out by now. However, there's no reason at all to to think he's a murderer."

" What, when he was there on the spot? " Owen said. " When he knew Tom Hearn? When he was in a perfect position to hand on information about local people? "

" Oh, Mr. Loader, how you do leap to conclusions," Mr. Barfoot said. " All kinds of people could have done that. As a matter of fact, you could have done it yourself."

Owen had just picked up one of the drinks that Mr. Galpin had put down on the rickety painted iron table around which we were grouped. Some of the gin slopped over on to the table, as Owen said, " I don't feel I'm in a position to take offence at anything anyone says to me, but please don't go too far, Mr. Barfoot."

" But I find it very interesting to study the different

aspects that the truth can be made to wear," Mr. Barfoot said. " Complete disguises sometimes, complete falsifications. For instance, I believe it would be quite easy, Mr. Loader, to make it appear that you murdered Tom Hearn. You drove Anne in to the post office on Saturday afternoon, but where did you go then? In that fast car of yours, you could easily have got back in time to do the murder. And your motive might have been jealousy. Believing, because of Jess's behaviour, that it was Peter you'd just seen, you might have gone back to settle what you considered your account with him. On the other hand, you might have had a different motive. You're a rich man, aren't you, and no one seems quite sure where your money comes from. And your own burglary could have been arranged to deflect suspicion from you. And meeting Peter Lindsay when you married your wife, you could have recognised how closely he resembled a certain cat-burglar of your acquaintance, and thought there were possibilities in getting the burglar to operate in a district where he would be taken for Peter. . . . Oh, there are limitless possibilities."

As the colour slowly drained out of Owen's face, and his firm mouth dropped open, Margaret sprang to her feet. " What abominable lies! " she cried. " A lot of people know where Owen's money comes from. It was made by one of his great-grandfathers, who owned most of a shipping-line in Glasgow. Furthermore, Owen's acquaintances aren't cat-burglars! "

" It's all right," Owen said with a wry smile. Then suddenly he moved towards her, caught hold of her hand and clasped it tightly. " I think there was meant to be a moral in Mr. Barfoot's little talk—quite a useful moral."

" Now that's something I never thought of," Mr. Barfoot said, studying his finger-nails. " A moral. If there's a thing I've always distrusted, it's a story with a moral. No——"

What happened then is only a confusion in my mind. Several things happened and to me it seemed that they happened all at the same time, although there must really have been some sequence in them. But even now I remember them all as separate sounds and pictures.

The ones that have remained clearest are Peter's shout and the way that he launched himself across the space between them straight at Owen, grasping him by the shoulders, bearing him backwards and down to the ground. I remember the shock on Owen's face, then the dazed anger. If he hadn't been taken completely by surprise, Peter would never have succeeded in bringing him down, for Owen was far the heavier and stronger.

I remember also what I suppose must have come first, though it was only afterwards that I realised that I had heard it at all. It was the crash of breaking glass and somebody shrieking and a curious little hiss of sound that went by me like a sharp breath on the still air of the afternoon.

Then I remember scared faces at the broken picture-window of the White Horse and as I recognised Sandra, struggling and screaming wildly in the arms of Mr. Biggs and Mrs. Galpin, events became a sequence once more and I grasped the astounding fact that Sandra had shot apparently at Owen and that he had been saved only because Peter had seen her in time.

Owen, still looking dazed but beginning to understand what had happened, was rubbing a bruised elbow and starting to mumble some inarticulate thanks, but Peter was already running towards the house, with Mr. Galpin close behind him and Mr. Barfoot, very red from the exertion and shouting some sort of warning after them, doing his best to run also. I started to run too, but Margaret stayed on the terrace, going down on her knees beside Owen.

As we came crowding into the bar, we saw that Mr.

Biggs and little Mr. Joe Cogley between them had Sandra
in a tight hold and that Mrs. Galpin was holding a
revolver in a wavering hand, well away from her body and
looking at it as if she expected it to writhe around in her
grasp and bite her. Three or four other people, standing
in a stupefied row against the wall, looked on with terror-
stricken faces.

As Mr. Galpin appeared, his wife turned to him,
thrusting the revolver at him and crying in a high,
shaking voice, " Take it, Arthur, take it! "

Even purpler in the face than usual, he put a hand out
for the gun.

As he grasped it and just as it seemed accidentally to
point straight at Sandra, Daniel Barfoot, a man whom
I should have believed incapable of using any weapon
but his tongue and his pen, reached for an empty beer
bottle on the bar, and brought it crashing against Mr.
Galpin's elbow. Mr. Galpin let out a scream of pain, the
gun shot out of his hand and went slithering across the
floor into a corner. His wife, all her helplessness disappearing, tried to reach it before Peter, but he was too
quick for her and spun round to face the room, the gun
in his hand.

I remember the hand was steady and he looked very
threatening, but somewhere at the back of my mind I
was sure that he had never fired any kind of gun in his
life and that in a moment the Galpins were going to
realise that and that then the thing in his hand would
become an embarrassment. So I moved up beside him,
and luckily he understood why, let me take the gun from
him and, following Mr. Barfoot's example, grasped a bottle.
He was just in time, assisted by two of the white-faced,
bewildered people standing against the wall, to prevent
the murder of Mr. Barfoot.

The strangers naturally did not know who required to
be protected from whom, so it was in a wary, distrustful

quiet that we waited for the police. A whispering little
trickle of evil words poured out from between Mrs.
Galpin's tight lips, mainly directed at Sandra, but she,
as the struggle ended, had suddenly sagged unconscious
in Mr. Biggs's arms and he had hurriedly laid her flat
on the floor, gone behind the bar and started pouring out
drinks for everyone.

Reaching eagerly for one of these, Mr. Barfoot sat
down, panting jerkily, and as Owen and Margaret came
in together, took up the conversation almost where it
had been interrupted.

" A story with a moral—no indeed, I was really just
clearing my own mind," he said. " Because, up to
a point, as I said, you made an excellent suspect, Mr.
Loader. But there was always the problem of transport.
Tom Hearn went to Dr. Lindsay's house on his motor-
bike, but he didn't leave on it, yet the bike turned up
in Lachester. So it looks as if the murderer went to the
house by some other means, then left on the bike, probably
wearing Tom's helmet and goggles. And though you
could have arrived by car, getting rid of the bike would
have presented difficulties. And that barred out Mr.
Biggs too, whose behaviour might otherwise have seemed
suspicious, because he was removed in a coma from the
lay-by and taken home by Mr. Cogley. I'd wondered,
before I heard Mr. Cogley talking, if the bike could have
been removed in the van. But apart from the difficulty
of loading it on to the van on a public highway, Mr.
Cogley told us that he put his own bicycle in there when
he drove the van away. So it seemed to me that although
the murderer probably went to the house by the van, he
left on the motor-bike. It wouldn't have been difficult
for Mr. Galpin to organise. Mr. Biggs, I believe, was
generally the last to leave here at closing-time. Some
knock-out drops could have been put in his last drink,
Mr. Galpin could have followed him out to the van,

pushed him to the side when he collapsed, put on his hat and driven off. The rest would have been simple, because Tom Hearn himself had opened the back door of the house, in case he needed a quick get-away. Mr. Galpin had only to go in, call him down and shoot, then ride off into Lachester and be picked up by his wife, returning from a shopping-trip in their own car. If he got into the car unobserved and hid behind the seat, no one need know that he had ever been out."

Mr. Galpin, now in the grip of Owen Loader and a plump commercial traveller, had been hissing words of rage to himself while Mr. Barfoot talked. At the same time, there was a look of petrified amazement on his face, as if he couldn't believe in what was happening to him.

Mr. Barfoot took a sip of whisky.

" I believe Sandra was really at the centre of the whole affair," he said. " With her passion for her husband and her violent nature, she was a much more immediate danger to Mr. Galpin than the police. And her mother objected, no doubt, to her being put out of the way at the same time as Tom. Mrs. May must have a certain influence over Mr. Galpin—sentimental, I assume, since her brains can't have contributed much to the success of the gang's activities. But hence the business of supplying Tom with some quite false information about Dr. Lindsay's jewellery and instructing him to burgle her house, while trying to get Mr. and Mrs. Lindsay out of the way in such a manner that Sandra didn't know where they'd gone and wouldn't believe their account of it. Sandra was to believe that Tom had been killed either by his brother, or in mistake for his brother."

Mr. Barfoot's glass was empty. He gave it a longing look, then resolutely pushed it away from him.

" It's still a problem why Tom had to be killed," he went on. " He was drinking, of course, and I believe his boasting had got him suspected of the burglaries down

here, and he'd taken to dropping in here too obviously,
so that Mr. Biggs, for one, knew him quite well by sight.
Naturally, Mr. Galpin wouldn't have liked that. And
Sandra probably knew it. She must have been very
scared at what she saw in Mr. Galpin's face when Tom
came in here, a week ago, and met Anne Lindsay. But
unluckily for Tom, she couldn't manage him. Besides
that, however, Tom had had a very good season, using the
information which Mr. Galpin must have been able to
pick up quite easily in here about the movements of people
in the neighbourhood, and making some big hauls. So
no doubt the Galpins hoped to hang on to most of his
share. Mrs. May, of course, would have had to be well
paid for her co-operation and Sandra given some compen-
sation, but neither of them would have known precisely,
as Tom did, what had been stolen. . . . Yes, I dare say it
appeared a good time to shut up shop, particularly when
chance sent a twin brother along, to become a scapegoat
for the murder, or at least confusingly involved in it.
Mr. Galpin certainly fostered their interest in each other,
handing on Peter Lindsay's address to Tom Hearn,
perhaps suggesting to Tom that he should explore the
possibilities of using his brother to create alibis for
him. . . ."

A shout from Mr. Galpin interrupted him. " Perhaps!
Probably! *If* I did this, I *could* have done that! I don't
know who you are, sir, but you're mad! You've said all
that in front of witnesses and what you're going to pay
when I bring an action for slander is going to make you
wish you'd never been born! "

" To someone with my unfortunate nervous system,
Mr. Galpin, that wish is sometimes bound to come without
your assistance," Mr. Barfoot said, picking up his empty
glass and looking at it dreamily. " This wonderful
drink, for instance—it's poison to me, you know, sheer
poison. I've been practically committing suicide before

your eyes. But apart from that, Ivy May will talk now. I don't know about Sandra. She may have a code which doesn't permit it. She may merely try to murder you again if you should fail to be convicted. It was, of course, you she was shooting at when the sudden movement of Mr. Loader towards his wife upset her aim. That was what I'd hoped to be in time to prevent—either her murder of you, or else your murder of her—but in the event, it was really Mr. Lindsay who prevented it. And I'm thankful he did. Poor Sandra doesn't deserve to become a murderess. But Ivy May will talk. Have no doubt about that. From what I've heard of her, I'm quite certain she's one of the people who always do a lot of talking when things go wrong."

There were the sounds of voices and hurried footsteps outside just then. Inspector Belden, pushing his way into the bar, saw me standing with my back to the wall opposite and gun in my hand, which happened to be pointing at him.

Like the brave man that he undoubtedly was, he rushed me, giving me a horrible fright. The whole situation took a good deal of explaining. Unfortunately, in the middle of it, Mr. Barfoot suddenly became doubled up with pain and told us all, between terrible groans, that he had perforated and was about to die.

For a little while it was very alarming, but Dr. Lindsay arrived and handled him successfully. I remember her telling him in her sharp, definite way that he had no right, in his condition, to go driving about the country, forgetting to eat at regular intervals and drinking spirits. If he would lead a reasonably quiet life and stick to his diet, she added, there was no reason why he shouldn't live to be ninety. He answered that ninety was too near to be interesting, and that if she wanted to impress him she had better make it a hundred.

At last all of us but the Galpins and Sandra were

allowed to leave. Mr. Biggs, driving unusually straight, departed in his van. The Loaders, silently absorbed in one another, drove away in the Jaguar. Dr. Lindsay insisted on taking Mr. Barfoot in her car, saying that after that attack, he was unfit to drive. Peter and I got into the Austin Seven.

I had thought, as we got in, that we were going to follow along behind Dr. Lindsay, but as Peter drove out of the car-park he turned the car in the other direction and started back to London.

I made a half-hearted protest. " Isn't your mother expecting us to go back with her, Peter? "

He shook his head. " I told her I was going to take you home."

" Didn't she mind? "

" When she's got your Mr. Barfoot to manage? " He grinned. Then the grin faded and he took a hand off the wheel to take tight hold of one of mine. " Oh, Anne, let's only mind about one another for a little while! "